T0137514

Big Elmer

TED E. HURLBURT

WESTBOW*
PRESS
A DIVISION OF THOMAS NELSON
& ZONDERVAN

WestBow Press books may be ordered through booksellers or by contacting:

WestBow Press
A Division of Thomas Nelson & Zondervan
1663 Liberty Drive
Bloomington, IN 47403
www.westbowpress.com
1 (866) 928-1240

Because of the dynamic nature of the Internet, any web addresses or
links contained in this book may have changed since publication and
may no longer be valid. The views expressed in this work are solely those
of the author and do not necessarily reflect the views of the publisher,
and the publisher hereby disclaims any responsibility for them.

Any people depicted in stock imagery provided by Thinkstock are models,
and such images are being used for illustrative purposes only.
Certain stock imagery © Thinkstock.

ISBN: 978-1-4908-4394-0 (sc)
ISBN: 978-1-4908-4395-7 (hc)
ISBN: 978-1-4908-4393-3 (e)

Library of Congress Control Number: 2014912196

Printed in the United States of America.

WestBow Press rev. date: 08/25/2014

Contents

Introduction vii

Chapter 1 1

Chapter 2 9

Chapter 3 20

Chapter 4 31

Chapter 5 35

Chapter 6 38

Chapter 7 42

Chapter 8 46

Chapter 9 62

Chapter 10 72

Chapter 11 84

Chapter 12 89

Chapter 13 92

Chapter 14 102

Chapter 15 111

Introduction

The story you are about to read is fiction. All of the events, characters, and descriptions are invented … except for Big Elmer. There was a man named Elmer who fit the description of the Big Elmer in this story. He was a giant of a man and a loving Christian, but the events of this book, to my knowledge, were not a part of his life.

As you read this story, four things can be seen.

1. No tragedy is so great as to overwhelm good.
2. We learn more from our failures than we do our accomplishments.
3. Success is often built on a foundation of misfortune.
4. Forgiveness begets forgiveness.

Laugh a little, cry a little, and enjoy a lot.

CHAPTER 1

Big Elmer had a pair of loving hands. They were the hands of a man with a loving heart, hands that would tell a wonderful and powerful story.

If anyone shook the hand of Big Elmer, as he was affectionately called, they would never forget coming in contact with a hand that was so broad and thick that it was like shaking hands with a baseball mitt. Big Elmer's huge hand was well in proportion with the rest of his preponderant form. He was the most muscular specimen of human power wrapped in a body that anyone could behold.

He was tremendously big boned. His facial features were huge and coarse. Shoulders were almost twice the breadth of the average man. By the size of his arm, one would think a foot should be protruding from the end rather than the hand. It was no wonder that there was a measure of timidity expressed in the eyes of those who met him. That timidity was immediately dispelled by his dancing eyes and bright smile. His handshake was from a loving heart that had been kissed by God's grace.

Big Elmer was recommended for enrollment to South Bay Bible College by Pastor Koch, who was a member of its board of directors. The school was a small ministerial training college that took pride in maintaining a close, informal rapport with their students. Dr. Price, a professor, had the opportunity of teaching these fine students.

In addition to his teaching responsibilities, he had been assigned to Student Services. He would book the music teams and fill requests for students to speak in local congregations. He strove to motivate students in areas where their talents could best be used. One of the rewards of his position was seeing the students mature in knowledge, zeal, and wisdom. It was in the latter area that he came to appreciate Big Elmer.

Not too long after first meeting Big Elmer, four or five students and Dr. Price were sitting on the lawn and talking about their last class session, which focused on the life of the apostle Paul and his conversion to Christ. Soon they were all sharing their own experience of becoming Christians.

Big Elmer stood up, lifted his massive hands, and turned them over and back, over and back, over and back. As they looked into the serious expression on his face, he began to tell the most fascinating and devastating yet wondrous experience of how he became a Christian. As he spoke, there was total silence, for Big Elmer had completely captured their attention.

He spoke slowly and softly, and they gathered more closely around the towering man so as not to miss a word. He told them about his hands, hands that were trained to conquer and to hurt. "Before I came to South Bay Bible College, before I met Christ, I crawled through the ropes into a ring to match my brawn and wit against another human being. Wrestling was my life, the object of my love. I breathed wrestling, ate wrestling, and my dreams were dreams of wrestling. It can really get ahold of a person. Everything about it, from the smell of the dressing room, the glare of the ring lights, to the response of the jeers and cheers of the crowd. These are the things I trained for, worked for, and yes, even lived for. I knew how to pretend to be hurt when I wasn't and how to appear to be permanently maiming my opponent while not hurting him at all. I was a proud man. Most of all, I was proud of my hands."

Big Elmer was still looking at his uplifted hands, still turning them over and back slowly. They all looked at his hands too. As they stared, the fingers slowly curled into two massive fists. The muscles of his arms rippled into hardness. His shoulders hunched, and his once dancing eyes now shot forth sparks of fire. His big happy smile moved into a snarl of hatred. They leaned far back as real fear crept into their hearts.

Elmer roared, "With my hands I could take a man's head and crush it!"

They all scooted back even farther.

The little group had grown to a dozen or more people. The girls were wide-eyed, their hands cupped over their mouths as they stood frozen in place. The guys looked with wonder and a weird kind of admiration.

As Big Elmer relaxed, so did those around him. His eyes twinkled. The big smile was again on his face. It was as though he had emerged from a dark fog filled with the bleakness of the past and now walked into the bright clearness of the now. Yet there were still shadows—shadows of self-blame, of guilt, of shame. They could tell that he wondered if the shadows would ever leave.

Elmer continued his story. "My last wrestling match was with a young contender. Billy the Kid was his ring name. He was just getting started in professional wrestling. He'd had maybe a dozen bouts or so, but I was the first big-timer he would wrestle. Prior to the match we talked over some of the holds we would do, about the length of time each would take before exchanging offense for defense, secret hand signals we would use so no one would get hurt.

"Billy the Kid was really excited and gung ho to have this match. I told Billy I would let him put on a good show before I took him down. Billy gave me a big grin and told me that it may not be him who has the last fall. I thought that Billy was a cocky kid, but that's what it takes in this game. I kind of liked him.

"The match was going pretty well. Billy was making a good show of it. It was evident that the Kid felt this was more than just a match. To him it was a golden opportunity to let the wrestling world know he was more than ready for the next level."

Big Elmer looked at his hands again and continued his story. "The Kid made a rookie mistake. Maybe it was because he miscalculated my speed. I moved in, elbows high. As we banged chests, my arms were around him and my fingers interlocked. I pulled him tight and applied the pressure. It was as good a big bear hug as I could have possibly achieved. I squeezed tight and held it, waiting for the secret hand signal to let up, but Billy the Kid made none. *Boy, this kid is really tough,* I thought."

They could tell that Big Elmer was struggling to get the rest of the story out. His speech was slowed by grasping for words, and his eyes welled up in tears.

Then Elmer continued by telling them of the biggest mistake he ever made in his life. "With a little jerk, I squeezed harder. There was a loud pop, then a scream of anguish. The kid lay limp in my arms. I could tell his back was broken. I lifted Billy in my arms and stared into his ashen face. Then ever-so-gently I laid him tenderly on the mat as though he were a newborn babe."

As the students and Dr. Price hung on his every word, their eyes were filled with both fear and sorrow mixed with admiration for the frankness and honesty that was pouring forth from Elmer's heart.

Elmer continued, "Confusion reigned supreme in the ring. The referee was the first to the Kid. Handlers and managers came from both corners. The ring doctor, with his little black bag, was next on the scene. Then a navy doctor came from the audience. This young female told the ring doctor that she had served on the hospital ship *US Mercy* and that she was an expert in bodily injuries.

"The ring doctor recognized the navy doctor, Dr. Koch, from Oak View Hospital and put her in charge.

"Dr. Koch, quickly and skillfully slid her hand under the Kid's back and then ran her fingers down his rib cage. 'Two separate fractures of the spine,' she announced to those in the ring, 'At least two ribs broken.'

"The ring doctor nodded. Dr. Koch added, 'He may have lung damage too.'

"Paramedics were now in the ring. She looked at them and snapped, 'No head brace! There is no damage to the neck. We don't want to place any pressure on the spine.'

"'Hurry up with the board,' she ordered. 'Strap him in at the ankles just above the knees, then around the pelvis and head, but no straps around his chest. And I mean no straps. Like nothing!'

"As the EMTs followed her directions, her last comments seemed less demanding. 'Good job. Well done. Now onto the stretcher, and don't spare the horsepower getting to Oak View.'

"As they were taking Billy out, the crowd stood and applauded, and each row turned to follow the precession out toward the locker room. There were no cheers, no boos, no vocal sounds at all, just their respectful applause.

"While all of this was going on, the referee came over to Hank, my manager, and whispered something in his ear.

Hank nodded in agreement and turned to me. 'Elmer, it's time to go. Let's get out of here now! Come on!'

"As I crawled through the ropes, I turned to look back. They were placing the Kid on a stretcher. The navy doctor was standing there, looking at me. Just as our eyes met, I was yanked away, Hank yelling at me, 'Watch where you're going, not where you've been. I don't want you going headlong down these steps. We don't have any stretchers left.'

"In the locker room I sat in a chair, my mind going in circles. Everything seemed all jumbled up. *What have I done? What am I going to do? Stop thinking about yourself, you idiot. Think about Billy the Kid.*

"My mind kept racing. *What happened? How did I miss his signal to let up? But I felt no signal. Did he give one? Even if he hadn't, I should have known. I should have known.*

"These and a dozen other questions were spinning in my head.

"Hank came over to me with water in a paper cup and a pill and said, 'Take this. The navy doctor tried to come down here, but I told her the locker room was for men only. She made me promise I would give you this pill.'

"As I stared at the pill, Hank continued, 'I asked her if it was a Mickey. She just laughed and said it would help you think straight. Here, I've kept my promise. What you do with the pill is up to you.'

"I took the water … and the pill."

Elmer took a deep breath and looked at the ever-growing crowd that was seated on the lawn. He noted their interest and amazement at the story about his conversion to Christ. Elmer continued, "Hank kept the reporters and others away. He even told the commissioner I would speak to no one that night. Hank made an appointment for the day after next for me to meet with the commissioner at their office.

"There was a long silence that Hank broke by saying, 'Get in to the shower, get dressed, and go home.'

"The shower felt so good. It made me feel clean. It felt good to get into street clothes again.

"Hank hadn't left, and I was glad he was still there. I informed Hank that I was going to make one stop before going home. I was going to the hospital and see how the Kid was doing.

"Hank pleaded with me, 'You don't have to do that, Elmer.'

"But I insisted and told him that I wanted to go alone.

"Hank understood he was more than a manager to me. He was a true friend. I knew he didn't want me to go alone, but he kept silent.

"I told Hank I would see him the next day and left."

CHAPTER 2

There must have been nearly thirty students seated on the lawn by now as others stood in the back.

Ira, a good-looking first-year student fresh out of high school, said, "Elmer, you don't have to go on with this if it's—"

The booming voice of Dr. Price interrupted, "Go on, Elmer. You need to tell us, and we need to hear."

Big Elmer nodded his head, lifted up one of those massive hands, drawing it back across his cheek to wipe away a tear. He took a deep breath and began to speak slowly in a soft, low voice.

"I was confused as I climbed the steps of the hospital. A distant clock struck the news that this awful day was over and a new day was beginning. Nothing could be worse than the day that had just ended, or could it?

"What would my coming here accomplish? I was torn with guilt. What could I say? How would the family react when the man who injured their loved one broke in on a private scene of grief, wonder, and sorrow? Would they yell at me? Would they think I was there to gloat over my victory in the ring? They could do nothing but hate and despise me."

"Then I had to ask myself, *Why am I here?* I had no reasonable answer. I was scared, trembling. I was ready to turn around, find a bar, and get good and drunk. But something ... or someone ... pushed me forward. With my next step the automatic doors to the hospital lobby slid opened.

"As I entered, I saw a rather sleepy-eyed receptionist and walked toward her. A smile came on her face as though she was glad to see someone.

"'May I help you?' she inquired.

"'Yes! Where have they taken the Kid?' I responded in a rather commanding voice.

"Her smile faded a bit as she replied, 'I'll need a better name than the Kid.'

"'Billy the Kid,' I shot back.

"The smile returned to her face. 'I'll need a last name, and if you tell me he's the bank robber, I'm calling security!' There was a twinkle in her eye that even brought a half smile to my lips. For the first time in hours I could almost smile.

"'Let me think. We don't use last names much. Uh, Redding maybe ... or Redman or something like that,' I replied.

"She looked over her list of patients and called the emergency room. As she hung up the phone, she looked over at me. She told me that the person I wanted was admitted to the hospital a couple of hours ago and was now in surgery.

"She was all business now. 'Take the elevator to your right. Go to the third floor, turn left at the hallway, and then take another left. At the end of that hallway is a waiting room. The family is there.'"

One of the young girls sitting on the lawn lifted her voice, which was filled with awe, and said, "You must have been driven by a great love and compassion, Big Elmer. You could have taken the easy way out and gone home. You must have been led by the Spirit of God."

Elmer nodded his head and continued, "When I reached the family, I found three men and a woman—all in their midforties—a teenage girl, and the navy doctor. I stood in the doorway motionless. Finally I blurted out, 'I'm … I'm Big Elmer.' That's all I could think to say."

"'Come in,' the woman said with a warmth in her voice that would have melted steel. 'This is my husband, Mr. Reeding, our daughter, Tammy, our two pastors, Pastor Gibbs and Pastor Koch, and his daughter, Dr. Katie, who has been an important part of our family since she was a young girl. We were all in the audience to see our son, Billy, wrestle.'

"Just then two doctors came in, still in their surgical garb.

"'We did all that we could, but we lost the battle. There was just too much internal damage, too much bleeding. His back was broken in two places plus other spinal injuries. Three ribs were broken, which did massive damage to his lungs and placed a great deal of pressure on the heart. We were fighting a losing battle from the start. We did all we could. There was just too much damage. They are cleaning him up now. As soon as they have finished, you can go in and see him.'

"'We tried to talk him out of wrestling," said Mr. Reeding, sobbing. 'But it is all he wanted to do. He wanted to make it his life's career, and it looks like he did.'"

Some of the girls seated on the lawn were weeping openly. The fellows took a deep breath, fighting back the tears. Even Dr. Price reached into his back pocket for a handkerchief.

Elmer also wiped a tear and went on with his story. "I spoke with heartfelt sorrow and said, 'I'm sorry. I'm so sorry.' I covered my face with my hands, as though I was trying to cover my shame.

"A nurse appeared and gave a nod to the doctors. They turned toward the Reedings. 'If you are ready, you can go see him.' Mrs. Reeding motioned to Pastor Gibbs to come with them, and they started a slow walk down a long hall.

"I sat down on a couch. Dr. Katie came and sat next to me. Her dad, Pastor Koch, pulled a chair around so that he could sit in front of me. He placed his hand gently on my knee.

"'Why don't you talk to us about how you are feeling? You need to,' Pastor Koch encouraged."

"I lifted my face out of my hands, and my watered-filled eyes were exposed.

"Whispering, I said, 'All that I was proud of I now hate. I hate wrestling. I hate myself. I hate my life. I hate my hands, yes, especially my hands. Hands that I made a living with are now hands that caused death. Why couldn't the kid have been a drunken bum or a rotten person? Why not a guy who was a real drag on society? But no, he was a clean-cut kid from a good Christian family with so much to live for. But now it's all gone. Why, if that kid's God is so loving and kind, did He allow this to happen? So much that was so good is wasted because of me.'

"I lifted my head, looked full into the eyes of Pastor Koch, and blurted out, 'You want to know how I feel? Well, I'll tell you plain and simple. I'm hurting deep, deep inside, and I hate myself. That's how I feel!'

"The soft, low tones I heard were from Pastor Koch—words of kindness, love and comfort. 'I don't hate you. The Reedings don't hate you. Their God doesn't hate you. God loves you, Elmer. He loves you so much that He came to earth as a man. We know Him as the Son of God … and we call Him Jesus. Jesus has much stronger hands than you do Elmer because His hands act from a heart of love. His hands were constantly doing good, never evil; always helping, never hurting; always lifting up, never throwing down. His hands give life, never death. Even when they became nailed-pierced hands, they showed us He is strong enough to lift our heaviest sorrows. Love is stronger than hate, Big Elmer. What you do with your life will determine whether Billy the Kid's earthly life was wasted or not. You know, Elmer? God sees the whole picture when we see so little. Maybe in time we will all see this deep shadow of death fade into a beautiful sunrise. When you take the Christ of love into your heart, your hands, too, will become hands that do good, not evil; bring happiness, not sorrow; helping, not hurting; lifting up, not throwing down because of God's grace. You can be the recipient of His grace. You can have His love. God will forgive you of all the wrong you have ever done, even the death of Billy the Kid. You see, Elmer, when you place your strong hand in His, Christ places His strong love in your heart.'

"We talked until dawn. I questioned every statement Pastor Koch made.

"I wanted to commit my heart to Christ, to this Jesus of love. I wanted my hands to be used by Him. I wanted nothing more than to be His servant. But I didn't know how. What am I going to do? Where will this lead me? How will I know what God has in store for me? Can I make such a commitment blindly? I needed more answers."

Dr. Price spoke more to those seated on the lawn than to Elmer and simply stated, "God does not reveal to us our tomorrows but gently leads us into them."

Elmer continued with his story. "Dr. Katie's voice was talking to me now. 'Big Elmer, you have already started on this journey of serving Him when you entered this hospital waiting room. You demonstrated true courage, real grit, and true compassion that is much deeper than your self-hatred and your self-pity. Your pride had to be broken completely, torn out of you to make room for His Spirit to enter into your heart.

"'Elmer, let me ask you a question,' she continued. 'If God loves you so much that He allowed his Son to die for you so that you might now have an abundant life that will lead you to an eternal life with Him, for that is His will for everyone, don't you think He is capable of answering the questions you ask about your tomorrows? God has a great plan for you as He does for us all. It will be made known by your walk of faith ... not by sight. Where we are on the face of this earth is not nearly as important as what we are doing where we are. If we think our steps are steps of sight, we will be continuing our walk in *our* strength and *our* pride, which leads to many falls. A walk of faith is a walk in the strength of His might.'

"She went on even more tenderly, 'We need a relationship with the one who walks with us. The first step of this walk is to accept God's invitation, to receive His gift, which is His Son as your Lord and Savior. God has made His move. Now it's time for you to make yours. The only question to be answered tonight is this: Will you accept God's gift of love and start your walk of faith?

"As she talked, I became more and more interested in what she was saying. I found myself weighing each word, each thought. To me her face became more like that of an angel than a person. I just sat there pondering all the events of the last ten hours. I remembered the smell and the sweet taste of victory when I clasped my hands in the bear-hug hold I had on Billy the Kid, which had turned into a fall filled with agony, one that now was going to change the course of my life forever.

"Looking right at Pastor Koch, I said with a conviction that startled me, 'Yes, I believe that God gave me a gift, and I want to accept His gift, His Son, Jesus, as my Lord and Savior. I'm going to need a lot of coaching since I know next to nothing about the Bible. Will you help me?'

"Pastor Koch replied, 'Yes, we will. We won't leave you setting on the edge of the baptistery, I promise.'

"I turned to ask Dr. Katie a question, but she was now standing with her back to me, her hands to her face. I guess she didn't want me to see an angel cry.

"Beyond her through the window, I noticed the sun just starting to peek over the distant hills. This was indeed the start of a new day."

Big Elmer paused for what seemed to be a long time. One of the boys on the lawn asked, "Elmer, there is more to this than you have told us so far. What happened next?"

"Yes, there is," said Elmer. "At the inquest there were lots of questions and way too much publicity. These things I did not fear. The commissioner and the promoters and even Hank had much to fear. Film of the match showed that no signal was given to me from the Kid to let up on the hold. The Kid was unprepared to wrestle someone with my years of experience. The Kid's death was one of those unfortunate ring accidents. I was free to go. But this did nothing to dissipate the shadow of guilt and self-loathing I carry. To my surprise, no disciplinary action was taken, not on me or Hank or the promoters.

"Hank and all my friends, everyone told me it wasn't my fault. I took little if any comfort from this.

"Hank said, 'Elmer, the best way for you to get over this is to get back in the ring as soon as possible. We could have the biggest gate ever because of all this notoriety.'

"'Whoa, wait a minute, Hank,' I said and stopped him in his tracks. 'I've got something to tell you. I've been in the lowest pits of hell. There in the midst of my pain and anguish, I met Jesus. By His strong loving hands I have been lifted up. My hand is in His hand, and where that pathway may take me I do not know. Nor do I care just as long as we walk together ... hand in hand. These hands will never again purposely hurt anyone, Hank. I will never, ever again step into a ring to wrestle.' I realized my voice was both firm and filled with determination.

"Hank was startled at the sureness and conviction with which I had spoken.

"He stared back at me and said gently, 'Okay, okay, you've been through a lot. Just step back for a couple of weeks and think about your future. I think you are a better wrestler than you will be as one of those Jesus freaks. There's no money, no fame in that racket. I'll call you when I've got something put together. We'll both be rich. I guarantee it. You are well on your way to being number one.'

"Hank looked at me in a bewildered sort of way as though he didn't understand, gave me a hug, and said, 'I love ya', big guy.' He turned and walked away.

"I made my way home. I was so tired that I flopped down on the bed, kicked my shoes off, and nearly slept the clock around.

I needed some down time, time to sort things out. Too much has happened too fast. I phoned Pastor Koch and told him I was going up to my cabin in the high desert for a few days and told him my feelings. 'If you don't hear from me, not to worry,' I assured him. 'I'll call you when I get back.'

"Instead he asked me to stop by his house before I left. He had something very important to give me.

"When I reached the house, I found dinner had been prepared. There were three place settings. Dr. Katie invited me to dine with them and excused herself while she got her father.

"'So good to see you,' Pastor Koch said with a smile as he entered the room. 'I'm glad to see you'll be eating with us. We have our big meal at about this time.'

"They both expressed their approval for my getting away for a time. I didn't realize how hungry I was and tried to think when I had last eaten. Who would have ever thought that I, Big Elmer, would ever feel comfortable eating with a preacher in his home? Incredible! My life had not been lived favorable to a minister's expectations. I didn't feel worthy to be at his table.

"When we had all finished, we retired to the study. There were three books on the pastor's desk.

"'These are for you, Elmer,' Pastor Koch began. The first one was a burgundy-colored leather-bound Bible with my name on it. The next was a Bible dictionary, and the third was a concordance. He told me that the last two books would be a great help to me as a new Christian in studying the Bible.

"For the next half hour he began coaching me on how to best use these books. As I was about ready to leave, he handed me a paper with some Bible passages to study. They were the first four chapters of Exodus and chapters 7, 8, and 9 in the book of Acts. He told me I was to look for any similarities between Moses, Saul, and myself.

"'When you come back, we'll talk about these chapters,' he said in parting.

"I left, admiring my little library, and drove to my cabin in the desert. It felt so good to get away from all the confusion of events and the stress of being around other people. But lurking was the ever-present dark shadow of guilt. I just wanted to be alone with God and His Word, to pour myself into prayer. I felt the tension slip away and a great peace take its place.

"I felt as though I had just taken my first training class in knowing the Bible. It was so great. I wanted more. I need someone to direct me, to answer the millions of questions that kept popping into my head."

Elmer wrapped up his story. "That's why I'm going to Bible College. To me, I'm in a new training camp. I'm here so these hands can learn how to serve."

Looking at his watch, he said, "Wow, it's time for chapel service. Come on! Let's go in." They all followed him. In their eyes Big Elmer stood ten feet tall.

CHAPTER 3

It was a bright spring day in mid-May years earlier when Katie Koch came bouncing down the stairs from her bedroom to the living room with raised arms and the biggest smile that brightened her face to an almost heavenly glow.

With a loud voice she burst forth, "Hooray, hooray, hooray! I'm seventeen years old this very day! This is the day I've been waiting for!"

Seeing her father, she flung herself into to his waiting arms. He gathered her close and held her tight.

His voice was just above a whisper, "I know, I know, and selfishly a day I dreaded to see. But seeing the depth of your happiness, those dreads have faded away. Come, I fixed your favorite breakfast—scrambled eggs with ham and pancakes."

As they sat around the kitchen table, downing their food, she told her father again the events that drove her to want to be a doctor.

She reminded him of the time when she was five and saved a little frog from the clutches of a cat. She carried the poor thing into the house so Mom could fix it. Mom told her if that thing got loose, she'd eat nothing but milk and toast for a week. Mom led Katie to the bathroom and from the medicine cabinet got a short stick with cotton on each end and a bottle of iodine. Dipping the swab into the bottle, she told Katie to hold the creature extra tight because he would not like this. And she was right.

Mom told Katie something she will always remember, "Sometimes we have to endure a little pain so that we may have a more perfect body. It's in the Bible."

It was not too long after that when Mom became ill, and Dr. Wayne was at the house a lot after she spent some time in the hospital. He came every day and was there the day Katie came home from school and they told her Mom had gone to be with Jesus. Katie remembered her mother's words. "Sometimes we have to endure a little pain so we might have a more perfect body."

Or the time she brought home a baby bird that had fallen … or was pushed out of her nest. Dr. Wayne Wainwright was here, and Katie asked him what to do. He said to keep the bird warm. He called a friend of his and got more information for Katie. In a couple of hours he was back with a birdcage, an eyedropper, and a small bottle of something that she would need to feed the bird every couple of hours or so.

"Keep me informed on how you get along with your doctoring of the bird," he said as he left Katie alone with the little creature.

She introduced herself to the baby bird as Dr. Katie. It was fun watching the bird grow. When she started flapping her wings and looked as though she could make it on her own, Katie took the cage out to the front porch and hung it on a hook. Katie could see the cage from her bedroom window. This was the bird's favorite daytime spot. Katie fastened the cage door open and then ran up to her room to see what the bird would do. It jumped up on a perch and looked out at the world without bars for the first time. The bird looked in every direction—up, down, side to side— and then turned and came back into the cage. She did this three or four more times. Then she took a leap, flapping her wings a couple of times. Then she spread them and made a prefect landing on the top of the fence. She looked back at the cage so proudly. She made a few more short trips and returned to her home.

The bird did this for a couple of days, and at dusk a male bird had joined her. She went promptly into her home to her little nest in the corner and invited him in. He came to the door, and then he flew to the top of the cage. They squawked and squawked at each other. Then he left her and flew to wherever he had his home.

At morning's first light he was back and more chirping began between them again. Then they both flew away.

The little bird never returned to the cage. Katie felt good inside.

She whispered to herself, "Katie, you're a very good doctor."

Doc Wayne, as all his friends called him, was at the house, and Katie told him how her birdie had left her cage with another bird.

"So she flew the coop, did she? Well good for her." With a twinkle in his eyes, Doc Wayne continued, "Doc Katie, congratulations on a job well done. Yes, well done. But if you want to continue to wear that title, you'll need some training. We in the medical field speak with a very large vocabulary. You'll need to learn the lingo. By the time you graduate from high school, I want you to be well on your way to being ready for your formal training in medicine."

Every week Doc Wayne would bring Katie little flyers or pamphlets on some subject. If Katie didn't learn all the information he gave her, he would make Katie study it some more before he would give her another. The pamphlets started out with simple information regarding first aid. But during the next six years he gave Katie information on the anatomy of the entire human body. She learned how the bone structure and the muscles are related to the nerves and how the blood flows internally and how the heart and lungs work together. The pamphlets taught her how nutrients get to the organs and how they all interact with each another to make a healthy body. All of this was not by accident. Katie believed everyone was made by an intellect far greater than humans could understand. Even though the body God had formed was magnificent, when He breathed into that which was formed from dust, man was created in God's image.

As Katie's mother used to say, "God is great, and God is good all the time. It's in the Bible."

There was one more event during Katie's junior high school days that proved to her that God had a purpose in her becoming a doctor. She didn't see it at the time, but God works far ahead of people.

About three years after the bird had flown the coop, Katie had just gotten home from junior high school. She changed into her jogging suit, placed a sweat band on her head, and went over to the window to see the sun setting in the western sky. Suddenly she heard the screeching of tires as a car was making a left-hand turn onto her street. Just as the driver was about to complete the turn, there was a big bang. The front right tire had blown out. The car yanked to the right and clipped the back left fender of Katie's family car, which was parked at the curb. Then it careened to the left and hit a car broadside that was coming from the other direction.

The sound of metal being crushed by metal and the dust and steam that rose from the tangled wreckage was a frightening sight. Katie stood there frozen by the mess she saw before her.

"I can help! I can help!" Katie heard herself say.

She turned and picked up a hand towel that was neatly folded at the foot of her bed. Katie grabbed her first-aid kit. As she ran down the stairs, she nearly collided with her father, who was standing at the kitchen door.

"What's going on?" he asked.

"Crash, cars, phone 911. We need help," was all Katie could manage to say as she sprinted for the street.

Katie got to the car that had been hit broadside. Then she ran around to the passenger side, which was not caved in. The door was starting to open, so Katie pulled on it too. Begrudgingly it swung wide. Inside was a man and women in the front, both shaken but unhurt. In the backseat was a young muscular boy in his teens and his younger sister. Katie recognized him from Sunday school. She knew him just slightly as he was a few years older than her. For the moment Katie couldn't remember his name.

"How are you doing?" Katie asked in as calm of a voice as she could muster.

"Oh," the boy answered. "I'm banged up a little … but my sister is cut real bad. Blood is squirting out of her arm."

"Are you strong enough to get her out here and onto the lawn, or do you need my help?" Katie questioned.

"I'm plenty strong," was his crisp reply.

Katie sat down on the sidewalk and told the boy to bring his sister to her. He laid her across Katie's lap … and none too soon. The little girl had lost a lot of blood. Quickly Katie tied a knot in the hand towel and pressed it. The girl's arm was punctured just above the elbow.

A man smelling of liquor came over to offer help, but seeing all the blood, he turned ashen and stumbled away. In the distance Katie heard the whine of sirens and prayed, "Oh God, give them wings." Her big brother was hovering over them, and Katie asked his sister's name.

"Tammy. It's Tammy. We call her Tiny Tam," he spoke in a low voice.

"Thanks, Billy." The forgotten name came back to Katie out of nowhere. "Billy, can you stay close and keep her talking? Tell her that it's all going to be okay. Just keep her awake," Katie stated.

A middle-aged lady knelt by Katie and said, "Looks to me like you could use another hand."

"Oh yes, I can! Here, where my hand is placed, press firmly but not too hard. Put pressure right here and lift her arm up so the cut is even with the top of her head," Katie answered.

With one bloody gloved hand, Katie snatched off her headband and stretched it tight around Tammy's upper arm and secured it. Then she went to her first-aid kit, took out the gauze, and folded it into about a two-inch square.

"Let's take this towel off, and we will make this look a little more professional," Katie said, looking at the kind lady who became her third hand. The puncture looked nasty, but there was only a trickle of blood oozing out. Katie grabbed a cotton ball placed it in the middle of the gauze. She placed the makeshift bandage over the wound and wrapped it tightly with tape. Then Katie eased off the pressure of her headband to allow the blood to feed Tammy's hand and fingers. Katie looked over at Tammy and asked her if she could hear her. With eyes half opened, Tammy nodded her head. "Great!" Katie responded. "We have everything under control. You are going to be just great. You were so brave. I'm so proud of you," Katie said as she lifted her head toward the heavens and thanked and praised God for His help, for His timing. Katie felt she was in way over her head, but He was there. "Yes, God, oh thank You, and You sent me such good help." Katie turned to thank the kind lady who had helped her so much, but she was nowhere to be found. *Who was she? Where did she go?* thought Katie.

When the paramedics rolled in, two of them came over to Katie, Billy, and Tammy. They gave Katie back her headband and placed a really tight bandage on Tammy's arm. He asked who was responsible for the patch job. Billy spook up, and in a much too loud voice and his finger pointed at Katie, he said. "She did it. She did it. She stopped Tammy from bleeding to death." He went on and on step by step. Katie felt the blood rush to her face. She didn't want this. She interrupted and said there was a kind lady who helped her and that above all God was here. Flashbulbs were going off, and Katie vaguely remembered them earlier; however, she was too engrossed in keeping Tammy alive to pay any attention. "Well," stated one of the paramedics, "Whoever did this saved this little girl's life. I'm going to put a couple of headbands in my ambulance."

While he was talking, Tammy was taken off Katie's lap and placed in the ambulance. When they got her safely in, they motioned to Billy to get in. Then off they went.

Two other ambulances arrived. Into one of them, Mr. and Mrs. Reeding, the parents of Billy and Tammy who had been in the front seat of the wrecked car, were whisked away. In the other a man in handcuffs and smelling of alcohol was toted off along with a policeman.

Katie turned to go home. All she was carrying was her blood-soaked towel, headband, and first-aid kit. As she walked toward the house, she began to tremble, shaking so hard she could hardly open the door. All Katie wanted was a hot shower, clean clothes, a hot cup of tea, and time to think and pray.

When she entered the house, Katie heard her dad talking with someone. She also heard a woman's voice. Katie sure didn't want to talk with anyone. Nor did she want anyone to see her in this condition. Katie sprinted up the stairs and straight into the shower. The shower felt so good. She felt clean afterward. The shaking had stopped.

Katie got dressed, but she was so tired. The cup of tea would have to wait. She flopped on the bed and was out like a light. Katie woke up to the sound of her dad's voice.

As he was leaving her room, Katie heard him ask if she was all right. A woman's voice was assuring him that Katie was just emotionally and physically drained and that she knew exactly how Katie felt. "What she needs is a little rest," Katie heard her say. She thanked Katie's dad for something and then said "I'll see you in church."

Katie was up and stirring about when she heard her father's voice again. "Katie, get down here right now and look what's on the news. Hurry!"

The early evening news was showing the story of the accident. The TV station's van was driving right behind the Reedings car to film an event of Mr. Reeding cutting the ribbon for the official opening of the new childcare center at the Oak View Hospital, and then the crash happened. All of the scenes of the accident and some of following events were on tape and now being aired for the first time.

Katie learned that Mr. William Reeding, Sr., his wife, Rose, son Billy, Jr., and daughter Tammy were the victims of the crash. Mr. Reeding was one of the leading citizens of the area.

Reeding Industries was a company with large government contracts with the armed forces dealing with machined parts. Almost everything that flies, floats, or runs uses parts from Reeding Industries. He was a great civic leader who gave a lot of money and time back to the community. The entire family was highly respected.

Now Katie understood why there was all this TV exposure. The treatment of Tammy had full exposure from the time that Billy set Tam on Katie's lap until they placed her and Billy into the ambulance. The video ended, but the commentary continued to tell about Mr. Reeding's value to the community. Katie's father was being interviewed. He talked about Katie being on the scene and about her determination to become a doctor. Then Mrs. Virginia Gillespie, the head of the nurse training program at Oak View Hospital, was interviewed.

"Why are they making such a big deal about me when all I did was tie on a tourniquet," Katie said with disgust.

Katie gasped when she saw Mrs. Gillespie. "That's the woman who helped me. And that's the voice of the woman in the kitchen talking with you, Dad. Why didn't she take over?" Katie asked in voice that displayed her confusion.

Katie's dad turned from the TV, looked at her, and spoke, "That's exactly the question I asked, and she told me she had no need to. You were doing everything by the book, and besides, she wasn't wearing a headband," he responded with a chuckle.

When the news ended, the telephone calls started one after the other. The doorbell rang. People from the church began pouring in, and then Mrs. Gillespie stopped by.

The next couple of hours were kind of wild.

To Katie, this was it! Now she knew that God was calling her to be a doctor.

CHAPTER 4

"Dad, the time has come for me to start to prepare myself to walk down the pathway God has put before me," Katie said solemnly. "Today I am seventeen. Today I will join the navy. After boot camp I'll go to the navy medical training school, one of the largest training schools in America. The best part is that it's just a stone's throw away from our home."

"'God is so good! Oh, God is good all the time,' Mom told me that was in the Bible, so that settled it," Katie said with authority.

She gave her dad a big hug as both their eyes filled with tears.

Katie was sworn into the navy, and she then went off to boot camp.

With boot camp behind her, Katie was to start her training. There were all kinds of tests from aptitude and personality tests to medical knowledge to physical exams.

When all the testing was over, she was called in to see Commander Rice, the placement officer. Katie entered his office, saluted, and stood at attention. He didn't look up from the papers on his desk. He just sat there studying them.

"We don't know where to place you," Commander Rice exclaimed.

Fear made Katie's heart jump. *Was I going to be washed out even before I got started?* Katie thought.

"You're seventeen years old?" he asked.

"Yes, sir." Katie replied.

"So you're a high school graduate, but you never enrolled in any type of college. Is that right?" He looked rather puzzled.

"Yes, sir!" Katie again replied.

"Then tell me, young lady. How in blue blazes did you acquire this much knowledge and understanding of the medical world?" the commander asked.

He was looking Katie straight in the eye. "Answer me that," he barked.

"Yes, sir, but it will take a few minutes, sir," Katie cautioned.

Sarcastically he replied, "Yes, I bet it will, and it had better be good."

Katie told him about everything from the healing of the frog and the bird to the car accident with the Reeding family and how Dr. Wayne Wainwright helped her all the years of her childhood.

At this point she was interrupted by Commander Rice, who had a big smile on his face. "Dr. Wainwright is known as Rear Admiral Wainwright around here. I served under him for almost ten years. There is no man I respect more than that man. I'll contact him and call you in again when we determine where best to place you in our medical school. Your story had better be straight. Dismissed!"

The very next day Katie was called back in and placed in the medical school to undergo a battery of tests before she could be assigned to classes. These test consisted of entrance exams followed by final exams of class after class. Day after day for eight to ten hours a day for ten days, Katie was mentally exhausted. The tests became more and more difficult, and the last two days she could hardly remember how she did it.

It was more than a week before Katie was called back to Commander Rice's office. During that time she was sure she caught a glimpse of Doc Wayne leaving the administration building.

Commander Rice stood up and with a very stern look said, "Young lady, the tests you took and the testimony of Admiral Wainwright has led me to conclude that what you told me was greatly short of what the facts revealed. I'm sold. You are a gifted and remarkable young lady. We have decided to dismiss you from taking the following subjects." He handed Katie the list of the subjects with the grades of the tests she had taken. "Here are the classes you will take. Nearly two years have been shaved off your training. You have a two-week furlough. When you return, you will be given a promotion, assigned to new quarters, and will report for your first class the next day. Congratulations."

"And one other thing," he continued. "You had better perform really well because a lot of good men have stuck their necks way out to arrange this. We did so because we all have confidence in you. You can go now. Dismissed."

"Yes, sir, and thank you." Katie saluted, turned, and hotfooted it out of his office. She all but ran to the base chapel, where she could pray. Katie gave a prayer of thanksgiving and praise. "God, You have given me a pathway to trod, but God, I need Your help to keep up with You!"

CHAPTER 5

The next five years were better than Katie could have dreamed possible. Classes went well, and she was able to take her year internship at the Oak View Hospital. Now she could wear the title of Dr. Katherine Koch, MD. She had completed step one in accomplishing her dream goal for her life. The next step was to use this training to lead people to the Great Physician. He and He alone could bring humanity from a sinful and sick world to a cured and cleansed relationship with God. Katie knew she still needed a lot of training, and her prayer to such a wonderful God was one of praise and gratitude for His guidance. Katie's trust in Him was complete. She would walk with confidence in whatever pathway lay before her because her life was surrendered to finding His purpose. Katie remembered again how her mother oftentimes reminded her in her early childhood that "God is good all the time. God is good."

Katie's first assignment was aboard the hospital ship *Mercy.* This is a floating hospital more than 890 feet long with 1,200 medical personnel members and twelve operating rooms fully equipped with all the most modern medical devices. Again Katie could see the guidance of God, as He kept opening doorways beyond her expectations!

The next four years were filled with excitement and the deep satisfaction of sharing her skills as a physician with thousands of people who were suffering from the disasters of nature and at the hands of religious bigots. But one thing was lacking. Katie was unable to share her faith in the Lord Jesus Christ as she wanted and needed to. When they sailed to Malaysia to the area of Kuching to aid the thousands who had been injured and made homeless by an earthquake, they were instructed not to bring up religion because the people of Malaysia were very sensitive to the subject. Any mention of religion could lead to violence.

The same thing happened as they sailed in the Andaman Sea, where they assisted those who survived the horror of a tsunami. They did a great deal of good in alleviating the people's physical suffering, but they could not address their spiritual needs. Katie so wanted to share with them the blessings of God's grace, a grace reached by faith in Christ rather than by works.

While Katie felt greatly warmed by doctoring their broken bodies, it broke her heart not to fully minster to their broken spirits. She prayed earnestly to God to put her in a place where she could do both. It was then that Katie made up her mind to leave the navy at the end of her tenth year, though she was grateful for the training and experience she had obtained.

CHAPTER 6

Katie took off her uniform and hung it in the closet. She got into civilian clothes. Surprisingly they fit pretty well. Katie went downstairs to have breakfast with her dad. "My first day home. Oh, how sweet," she stated.

Katie's father made an announcement, "Katie, I want you to meet Thomas Walters, the president of South Bay Bible College. He and Doc Wayne have a proposition to offer you. So we have a lunch date at your favorite restaurant set for 12:30 p.m. today."

"Boy! You don't let any grass grow under my feet, do you, Dad?" Katie returned. "There goes another furlough. Oh well, what else is new?" she continued with a smile.

Katie was introduced to Brother Tom, the president of the college. She would never have pictured him in such an important position. He looked more like a farmer or a factory worker—very down to earth, not the potbellied, baldheaded, stuffed shirt that she had envisioned. His countenance radiated love and confidence. His words were positive and filled with understanding that immediately caused one to respect him as a true man of God.

Lunch went well and when they were nearly finished, Doc Wayne spoke, "Katie, Brother Tom and I want to offer you a plan. After talking with your father, we feel it will help you in fulfilling your desire to aid mankind through your profession and fulfill your vow to serve God. I'll offer you the first half of the deal."

"I'm seventy-five years old," he began. "My practice has been declining over the past two or three years. I plan to retire in two years, but before I do, I need someone to help me with my practice, someone whose integrity and skills are above reproach. I have helped groom you for this occasion since you were a little girl, and now I want to cash in on my efforts. I'm offering you a partnership with me until I retire, and then it's all yours."

"But before you give an answer," he concluded, "Brother Tom has the other half of the package."

Katie was overwhelmed! She jumped out of her seat, ran to Dr. Wayne, and gave him a big kiss on the cheek. People in the restaurant gazed in wonderment at her behavior, but she couldn't care less.

Katie started to say something, but Dr. Wayne interrupted her, "No words from you, young lady, until you hear the other half. Then you can talk."

"Yes, sir," Katie said and returned to her seat.

Brother Tom started in a soft voice. "We at the college take pride in training eager Christians in being as skilled in Bible knowledge and the communicating of that knowledge as well as you have been trained in the medical field. Here is what we are offering—an offer with as much benefit to our school as it will be to you. First you will need training in the Scriptures. This will be done for you through our correspondence department. In addition, there will be some class time that will be available to you. In return, you will spend one half day a week on campus as our campus doctor, donating your medical service for our faculty and students. Dr. Wainwright has been doing this for years and has an office and examination rooms already set up. He can tell you more about this. This will be good for both of us. You will gain from our expertise as we gain from yours. Between the demands of the college and Dr. Wayne, you will not have much time for any social life. You will really be pushed."

Katie was wide-eyed and seemed to be looking past the two men she was dinning with. Yes, even beyond the walls of the restaurant. Her voice had a bit of a quiver to it when as she turned her eyes toward the ceiling and said. "God, I did not think it was possible for me to love You any greater, but You have heard my prayers so many times uttered as to how I earnestly desired to spend my life in service for You. I know where You have led me over the years, and now God, the doors You keep opening are just too overwhelming. I don't understand why You are so good to me time after time. Again I am emotionally overpowered by Your loving grace." Katie paused and asked them when she could start.

Brother Tom answered, "Be in my office at 9:30 tomorrow morning. We will give you some tests, set up a curriculum for you, and enroll you to start the fall semester, which begins on August 30. Our school year ends the last Friday of May."

CHAPTER 7

Over the next ten months time just seemed to fly by. Katie was overjoyed by the ease with which she was accepted by the nurses, the staff, and the people who came into Dr. Wayne's office. Dr. Wayne did a wonderful job in announcing Katie's joining the practice with newspaper stories and an interview by the local TV station. She was the talk of the town—the local girl who came home from the navy to start her practice. One would have thought she was some type of a hero instead of just one of many doctors on board a naval hospital ship.

After the first week they added more office staff. Her appointment book was nearly full. A younger clientele began making appointments. Her practice grew by leaps and bounds.

A week before Memorial Day, Dr. Wayne pulled Katie aside and asked her if she would like to go see Billy Reeding have his first big-time wrestling match? He was really excited about the opportunity to wrestle with such a renowned wrestler so early in his career.

Katie responded, "I would love to. I was talking to him and his parents about it Sunday at church, and they were looking forward to it. But his mom and dad were somewhat apprehensive as I guess any parent would be. Oh, by the way my dad and a good number from the congregation will also be there."

"Be sure and wear your navy uniform. I'm wearing mine, as there will be a special tribute given to all a service personnel in uniform, and we get in free," Dr. Wayne said with a big smile.

Indeed this was a big night for Billy. He was given tickets to the bout for his family and special friends. We were seated in the third row. The first row was filled with reporters, radio and TV personnel with their equipment, and noted civic leaders. The memorial convention center was filled to see their *hometown* hero come up against Big Elmer, one of the top three wrestlers on the pro tour.

The convention center was set up like an arena with the wrestling ring in the middle. There were grandstands on all four sides with an aisleway at each corner. Katie, the Reeding family, Dr. Wayne, Katie's father, and the rest of the group had no sooner been seated when an announcement was made for all service personnel and veterans who were in full uniform to go to room 101W. Dr.

Wayne and Katie excused themselves and went searching for the room. There they were divided into four groups each behind a color guard of six. Each one was in the uniform of their branch of service where he or she had served and carried the flag of that service. One carried the lead flag of their great nation, Old Glory. They were to go double file.

An old sailor who was walking with a cane stood by Katie. He asked Katie if he could go in with her. She looked at the ribbons he was wearing and the medals that had been given to him, and she realized he had been at Pearl Harbor on December 7, 1941, and at the battle of Midway, which was the beginning of the end of a long and bloody war in the Pacific.

They marched down toward the ring. As the hymn of each branch of the armed service played, the veterans of that branch stood up. They were all in place, completely surrounding the ring as everyone sang the national anthem. The old man on Katie's arm had a tear in his eye. She felt so honored to have him escort her to the ringside. What a hero. He gave so much so that the nation could be free. He was truly a part of what is referred to as "America's greatest generation."

With the preliminaries over, they first introduced Billy the Kid. As he climbed into the ring, the crowd was on their feet. The roar was deafening. Then came Big Elmer. The greeting for him was less enthusiastic with a few catcalls mixed in. The combatants met in the center of the ring, and the referee said something Katie and the others could not hear. Both wrestlers nodded and returned to their corners. The bell rang. The match started and ended all too soon with the horrible heartbreak that led to Billy's death.

CHAPTER 8

The weeks seemed to fly. At South Bay Bible College both the student and faculty esteem and deep Christian love for Big Elmer grew. He was indeed a big man—big-hearted, generous, and gentle. When he was around, one felt lifted up and exhilarated. He talked more with his smile than he did with his lips. He demonstrated his faith more with his hands than he did with his voice so that when he did speak, he commanded attention.

One of the spring projects at the college was to go into the slum area and start a Bible study for the kids. Two upperclassmen were selected, and they were excited about the opportunity. Both were great students who came from fine middle-class families and had never been to the other end of town. As a matter of fact, the two had been warned by their parents when they were just kids to never go into that area. So it was with some trepidation that they ventured into the "Sodom of the city," as they called it. They made some friends, but some of the contacts they made were indifferent at best. Some were even hostile. The two warriors came back seeking other places where they might fit better in their quest to serve the Lord.

Big Elmer got wind of this. He asked about what they had encountered. When they told him, he said that he would like to give it a try.

"I think I might be able to reach them," he ventured.

There were no words of encouragement. "It's impossible to reach them for Christ. They are too content with their sinful ways to even listen, let alone accept the gospel message," they said.

Big Elmer replied with a big smile, "Yeah, it would be hard, but I can't get out of my mind how Jesus went to the cross for them as much as He did for us. There must be some way for them to know that they can step into the light of God's grace."

He turned and left.

The next stop was Dr. Price's office. He was teaching a class that would be over in about ten minutes.

Good, Elmer thought. *That will give me time to get my ideas organized.*

Fifteen minutes passed before he came in.

"Hi Elmer, what can I do for you?" he asked.

Elmer looked right into his eyes and said, "It is my understanding that the slums area Bible studies have been scrapped. If that's true, then I want to go in there and get the Bible studies and a lot more started ... like next week."

"What makes you think you can do this when two of our finest students have failed?" Dr. Price sharply replied.

"Glad you asked," Elmer continued. "I know how these folk think, how they feel, and what they really want because I grew up in the slums. I know how they feel about an outsider coming into their territory, trying to change them. The approach that was taken, though noble, is about 99 percent wrong. For instance, going in to start a kids' Bible study will backfire. Why? Because the kids will get all hyped up about Jesus go home and wonder why Mom and Dad never told them about Jesus, and the parents become defensive, scolding them or forbidding them to return to the Bible study. Starting with the kids can be counterproductive for a long-term effort. Oh, the kids must be reached. but it would be better to go for the men first. Go for the head, and the body will follow. But how can we reach the men? Make them realize their importance. Almost all of them were made to feel inferior by the men living in the suburbs. When we go into their area and offer something free to them, it makes them feel dependent on us, which in the long run increases their distrust of us. We must honestly look at them as God does. He is no respecter of people. He knows how beautiful we all are, and He sent His Son to die for us all so we could experience that beauty. We must accept the poor as better than we are and understand their thinking, and there is more."

"Yes!" replied Dr. Price with new interest in his voice. "Just how do you plan on doing this, Elmer?"

"We will start with baby steps. Ira and I will go there Monday and look around and see what doors God opens for us. I've got the brawn. Ira has the brains, so we make a good team. Monday ought to be interesting," Elmer stated.

"Go with my blessing and prayers. I'll be most interested in hearing about your adventures," replied Dr. Peirce with a hint of a smile on his usually stoic face.

Monday morning was a gray day with the off-shore clouds covering the sun. But according to the weatherman, it would slowly burn off, and by early afternoon it would warm up. They climbed into an old pickup with a faded sign painted on each door that read, "Jacks Tree Trimming," and a phone number that was of no value since Jack had quit the business about four years ago.

"Where in the world did you get this old clunker?" Ira asked.

"Oh, I bought it Saturday from an old friend of mine. It runs good but just doesn't look too sharp. Just what we'll need for the job we are going to be doing. Sure beats showing up in a new Caddy. We need to be accepted by these people, and we won't do it with a highfalutin appearance or attitude. We've got to look like them, talk like them, but always remember who we are and why we are here," Elmer answered.

"This is going to be fun. We will go as far and as long as God opens door for us. Every person we contact God has a purpose for our meeting them, and that purpose is to bring them back to Him. I just pray we will not fail. I know God won't," Elmer replied.

Elmer handed Ira a map and a red marker. He explained to Ira what they were going to do. "We want to drive up and down every street in the slum area and case it out until we find just the right spot to start reaching out to the wonderful people of that great area."

So they started out on a journey to the darkest, dumpiest, toughest part of town, believing that Jesus died on the cross for them as much as He did the rich and famous. They believed there was nobody too mired in the pits of sin who could not be rescued and kissed by God's grace.

As they drove they were surprised at the buildings that were closed, boarded up, and in disrepair. Some of the many vacant lots had charred ashes and foundations where buildings once stood, victims of riots a decade ago.

They came to the corner of Fifth Ave. and Main Street, where there was just one huge building on a corner of the block. The balance of the block was messy, trash-littered field where the remnants of buildings once stood. A Realtor's sign was on a window, and the same Realtor sign was seen on the empty lots. Ira wrote down the name, address, and phone number of the Realtor.

They got out and walked toward the building. Elmer would have loved to see inside. But the windows were boarded up, and even when he cupped his hands to a small crack, it was too dark to see anything.

"I sure would like to go inside and look around," said Ira.

Across the street from the large building a cafe was open. Next to it there were a couple of more shops and a small mom-and-pop grocery store that was owned and operated by a couple in their late sixties who had been there for more than thirty years.

"Let's cross the street and get a bite of lunch at the Main Street Café. It's almost one o'clock, and I'm getting a tad hungry," Ira suggested.

"Good idea. We can get a little flavor of the community and maybe some information too. I wonder how the cafe can stay open."

We entered the café, and Elmer spotted three men seated in a large semicircular booth in the rear of the room. A fancy clock, which looked out of place, hung above the booth and chimed the hour. Ira looked at his watch and noted it was a minute slow. A young lady whose name tag read, "Sandy," came out from the kitchen.

"You can sit anywhere you want. We just finished with our big lunch-hour crowd," she said with a whimsical smile.

Elmer and Ira pulled up to the middle seats of the counter that stretched across the front of the eating area where they could watch the three men in the mirror. As the two were going over the menu, Sandy spoke up and told them the cook had left for the day. They could have some hot soup and sandwiches, and the grill was still on. They nodded.

Elmer asked, "What kind of soup?"

She replied, "Tomato or chicken noodle. I can give you the chicken noodle at half price since it is kind of old and we're going to dump it when we close."

Ira spoke up, "I think I'll skip the soup and have a grilled ham and cheese on wheat."

"Smart choice, and what's your name?" Sandy asked.

Ira told her, and she replied, "Gee, that's a name you don't hear much anymore. I like it." She gave Ira a big smile.

"Now big boy, it's your turn. What will it be for you, whatever your name is?" Sandy asked.

"It's Elmer, and I want the Ruben on rye, grilled. I like you because you are honest. You tell it like it is," said Elmer, never taking his eyes off hers.

She never left his gaze but met it head on and replied, "Men call me a lot of things but never honest. Thanks. I needed that. Ham and cheese and a Ruben coming up."

Sandy turned to fix their lunch and in a few minutes brought them their sandwiches. As they were eating, Elmer looked in the mirror and saw the three men stand up. Two of them left the café, and the other one started walking toward them. Elmer swung his chair around and with a big smile looked at the man striding toward him.

"Hi, I'm Ross, the owner of Main Street Café."

"Hello, I'm Elmer, and this is my friend Ira." Elmer said no more than that, much to the surprise and disappointment of Ross.

Both men stood with their eyes locked on the eyes of the other. Elmer saw the expression in Ross's eyes begin to change. His face began to show uncertainty and even a bit of fear.

It was Ross who broke the silence. "I saw you drive by here three times in that old truck this morning. On the fourth time you stopped and walked all over the lot, even stepping it off to get the size of it. Then you walked all around the building to try to see inside. What's your game? You're not a cop, are you?"

"No, in no way am I affiliated with any law enforcement agency, and I'm no longer in any gaming business," Elmer replied.

Again Elmer stopped way short of what Ross expected.

Then Ross said, "So then you must have heard about me. I have five mares in my stable and use some of the area in the back of the building to board them. Most of the area is off limits. Used for storage maybe. If you want to ride one of my mares, it's $150.00 an hour. They're all good, and they're all clean."

"If the mare's name is Sandy, then we have a deal. Here is $75.00. That's your split, right? I want Sandy to show us the inside of the building. We'll take good care of her and return her better than she's ever been, if that arrangement is okay with her?" Elmer softly said.

"Do I have a choice?" she whispered as though she was obeying with much misgiving. Her smile was gone. Her eyes had hardness in them. She whipped off her apron, and as she turned toward the mirror, she fluffed her hair and said, "Okay, boys, follow me."

Elmer was still studying Ross. He stood, slumped shouldered, head slightly bowed. He was a very downhearted, lonely man who didn't like at all what he had to do to keep his cafe open.

The three crossed the street and began to walk down a long, wide driveway that ran all the way down the side of the building and separated it from the huge lot next to the building. Elmer found out that the driveway turned and went across the back of the building and emptied out in Fifth Ave. There were loading docks across the back of the building.

Just as Sandy was unlocking the door, Elmer said to Ira, "This building looks in good shape. I didn't see any dry rot or evidence of termites."

Sandy snapped her head around, and almost in tears and with a lot of anger, she spoke her mind. "Great! Great, you don't think much of me. Dry rot and termites is all you think about. They have a higher ranking than I do. Boy! That really turns me on. Do you think I like doing this? Well, I don't! But I need a place to sleep, and I do like to eat—two habits I can't seem to break. Come on in. Ross got his money for doing nothing. Well, I'll earn whatever you two give me. I know I'm dirtier than dry rot and lower than a termite. But there is only one thing lower than me, and that's the guys who use me. My dream, my hope, and my prayer is that someday I can get out of this racket. Let's get this over with now that we know where each of us stands."

Elmer stepped forward, blocking the entrance, and in a soft compassionate voice, he spoke, "Sandy, we know where you stand because you are a very honest person as I surmised when we ordered lunch. I appreciate that and think very highly of you. Sandy, there are only two things I have asked from you. One was a Ruben sandwich on rye, and the other was to see the inside of this building. I want something more for you, not from you. That something is for your hopes and dreams to be realized and your prayers answered, nothing more."

Sandy gasped and looked at Elmer with new admiration. She could not have predicted the day's events! "What are you planning to do here?" she asked.

Ira added, "You, Sandy, are an answer to our prayers. We prayed that the people we meet would be of God's leading, and He led us to you. We are looking for just the right location to start up an enterprise where this community can work out their problems together and have a better life than they have ever had."

"I think there are hundreds in the area who feel about themselves as you do and have the same dreams and hopes that you do. We just need the right location to start a dream factory and a hope store, and I think we have found it. Let's go inside and take a look," Elmer told her.

"They do. They do," Sandy said. She moved with a new purpose and stopped at a side door a little more than halfway down the length of the building, and before she unlocked the door, she turned to them and said, "This is a very small part of the building. This is where we girls work." Elmer and Ira saw two restrooms, showers, a waiting room, and five curtained-off areas. Sandy continued, "That's all I can show you, the rest of the building is strictly off limits. I have never seen it and have been told to act as though it doesn't exist. But now that I know what you want to use it for, I think I know a way for you to get a peek inside. See the door over near the corner of the setting room and the transom window above it? If you can get up to it, you might see some of what is inside, though the window is really dirty."

Elmer smiled at Sandy and then turned his attention to Ira and said, "Ira, get behind me and when I squat a little, jump on my shoulders and be sure you have your notepad and pencil ready. When we get to the window, do not touch it. Don't try to wipe away the dust. Just look and write what you see. Okay, up you go."

Elmer had a firm grip on Ira's ankles as he walked toward the window as though he was carrying no weight at all.

Ira was surprised as he gazed in wonderment of the bigness of the building. The open area was tremendous. His mind was in a whirl as he thought of all the possibilities this building held. Then he turned his attention to the contents of this huge area and began writing. He paused, took another look, and wrote some more. He did this at least a half dozen times and then announced that he was finished and was ready to be let down. There were two long rows of white wooden boxes about five feet long stacked three deep, and next to them were four rows of boxes about fifteen inches square. Because of the angle Ira had, he could not make out much of what was printed, MM on the long boxes and AM on the square boxes. A pathway separated them from the next collection of larger boxes, which Ira could see two lines of printing. On the top line were the letters RO, and the bottom line had LU. Along another pathway were more large square boxes. Ira saw the top line of these boxes had printed PR, and the bottom line had GR.

Twenty minutes had flown by before Ira's feet again touched the floor. He handed his notepad to Elmer, who read it and then reread it as though he was studying every small detail.

He turned to Sandy and said, "Sandy, you have never been inside the large portion of this building. You don't know what if anything is in the building, and that's just the way we are going to keep it. It is not that we don't trust you. It is for you own safety that it has to stay this way."

Elmer planned to return in a few days and would like to have access to the building. He wanted to take measurements and see about leasing the property.

"Here is my address and phone number and seventy-five dollars for showing me the building and twenty for the lunch. Keep the change," said Elmer.

Sandy timidly took the money, staring back and forth between Ira and Elmer. She almost smiled.

"I'll need the phone number of the café so I can keep in touch with you and Ross. We will be in need of you both to help make all of our dreams become a reality. But before we go, I want to have a time of prayer," Elmer declared.

Ira and Elmer prayed a prayer of thanksgiving for leading them to Ross and Sandy and for the property. They prayed also for wisdom, for using His blessings for His honor and glory.

Sandy stood, staring at them with of a somewhat bewildered expression. A tear was welling up in her eyes, and in a soft voice she said, "I don't know what's happening here, but before I always felt sick and dirty when I left that building that my life was just a gob of trash. Now for the first time since I was a kid in Sunday school, I felt a warmth, peace, and hope. Please, please don't let me down. I need your help. I've got a huge mountain to climb, and I can't do it alone."

Elmer took her hand and placed his hand softly on her shoulder and spoke so tenderly, so reassuringly. "We won't let you down, Sandy, and you will climb your dream mountain. And at its top you will realize how big and bright is the reality of your dream. Do you want us to go back with you and talk to Ross?"

"No, no, that would be bad. He would think that you were stealing me away to start your own stable and would hate us both and would be out to destroy us. I know how to handle Ross. You do your thing, and I'll do mine. When you come back in a couple of days, he will want to see you. Trust me," said Sandy with a confident and determined voice. She turned and walked back toward the café.

Elmer turned to Ira and said, "Before we go back to the college, I want to buy a few groceries and meet Mom and Pop."

They got into the truck, drove a block, made a U-turn, and parked in front of Mom and Pops Grocers. As the two were going in, they noticed a shoe shine stand looking like it had not been used in a long, long time.

Inside Elmer and Ira found a very clean store, well stocked with the essentials for eating and cleaning but very few extra items. Pop, a slight gentleman with thinning gray hair, was over at the meat counter near the back of the store, filling an order for a couple of pounds of ground round. Mom, a plump woman with slightly graying hair and a kind and loving motherly countenance, was at the checkout counter, talking on the phone and writing down an order.

Over the next few weeks Elmer and Ira would learn to love and appreciate this couple. For many years the couple had done favors for their customers, even developing a credit system so that they could eat and pay later. They even acted as a bank at times. One lady's husband was a compulsive gambler, and she would bring in his paychecks, cash them, and have the couple keep most of it. She would get groceries with her prepaid funds, and in a couple of weeks when her hubby would again get paid, they would reconcile the balance and start anew. Mom must have had more than a dozen of these kinds of prepaid accounts. She also had twice that many of "eat first, pay" later accounts.

When Mom hung up the phone, she turned, and after she apologized for keeping them waiting, she inquired, "How can I help you?"

Elmer told her what they wanted. She wrote it down, called Mae, a young girl who worked for her, and handed her their list. No words were exchanged. Mae just took the list and basket and went to fill their order.

Mae returned with the items the men had ordered, placing them on the counter. Mom handed her the list she had written down from the phone call. Mom kept her hand on Mae's and pointed to one item on the list, held up three fingers, made a fist, took Mae's hand, and softly pounded her palm three times. Mae looked again at the list, pointed to the item, and mimicked what Mom had done. They looked at one another, each smiling, and gave a nod. Mae then turned, basket in hand, and was off to fill the list.

Mom gave her attention to Elmer and Ira and simply stated the obvious, "Mae cannot hear or speak, but she is anything but dumb. She is as smart as a whip. We don't know what her IQ is, but it has to be in the upper bracket."

Mom kept on talking, telling them the account of how Mae came to work in the store. It was a fascinating story. "Mae was riding a horse. It got spooked by a gunshot of a hunter on her father's ranch in Northern California. She was bucked off and struck her head on a rock. She was unconsciousness for a couple of weeks, and when she did come to, she had lost all of her hearing. Not a good way to celebrate her seventh birthday. That was about ten years ago. She is capable of speaking but hasn't said a word since she lost her hearing. Then about three months ago her parents drowned in a boating accident. All of the few relatives she has live back east and did not want to be burdened with some deaf girl they had never met. She will not tell me where in Northern California she lived or how she got here. About two months ago she came into our market. She was in rags, hair dirty and unkempt. She plunked a quarter on the counter, pointed to herself, rubbed her tummy, acting like she wanted something to eat. I wondered if she could read and thought it was worth a try. I wrote on a notepad and pushed the pencil and pad toward her, pointing to the pencil. That started a series of notes back and forth

The last note I wrote stated that we live upstairs above the market and we had some homemade ham and bean soup and cornbread, and I invited her up to eat with us. But first she would have to stop at the bathroom, take a bath, and do something with that mop of dirty hair. I gave the note to her. Mae took the note and looked at it, and her eyes filled with tears. With both hands on the counter, head down, her body shook as she sobbed. I went around the counter and put my arm around her as we both went upstairs." Mom completed her story and then said, "So that's how Mae came to work for and live with us."

CHAPTER 9

During the next forty-five minutes as they were driving back to the college, Elmer and Ira went over step by step the details of the adventures of the day.

Ira said, "Now I know what we want to do inside the building. I'll draw up some plans for you to study. I'll see how much of the things we talked about can fit into the area. Let's see if I have everything—an all-purpose area that we can use as a chapel, fellowship hall, and eating area; a large commercial size kitchen; and a cafeteria with four to eight food counters. All of that can go across the front and should take up about a third of the space."

As they drove into the parking area of the college, they saw Katie nearing her car, gave a couple of toots on the horn, and waved at her to hold up. They parked, and she came walking toward them.

"Well, how did things go?" were her first words to them.

"This is going to take a while. Let's go in your office where we can set down. We'll tell you all about our adventures," stated Elmer.

Ira excused himself and walked toward the dorm. He had to study for an upcoming exam.

Dr. Katie's office at the college was small. The furnishings consisted of three chairs, an examination table, cabinets over and under a counter, a small changing area with a chair, and a shower curtain that could be pulled for privacy.

Elmer went over all the details of the morning and shared with her. Elmer showed her Ira's notepad and started to explain to her what was in the boxes.

Katie interrupted Elmer by reminding him that she had spent nearly eight years in the navy and knew full well what was in the boxes and only too well the havoc the contents could render. "Elmer, let me have Ira's notepad, for I know just who can handle this situation," stated Katie.

"I bet you do," said Elmer. "That's why I gave it to you. Once the *situation*, as you call it, is corrected, then we can move right in and continue to bring Christ into the area. The more people who have Jesus in their hearts, the more the cancer that has killed that district will dissipate. That is our mission. I pray that soon, very soon we can really go full speed ahead, having rid the area of the presence of organized crime."

Katie, with a deeply concerned and almost tearful expression, replied, "Oh, Elmer, my dear Elmer, you are running up against power and really nasty men. Please, please promise me that you will be careful."

Elmer looked deeply into her eyes and replied, "You are so beautiful that it is very hard for me to deny your request, but being careful will not accomplish the goal that I have for those living in slum areas. It will take boldness, much boldness to take Christ to them. They live in the fear of the mob. If they see even a hint of fear in me, I have lost the battle of showing them the pathway to freedom from what they fear. My trust and confidence in God is what allows me to walk through the valley of death and not fear evil. If I am doing His will, He will guard and protect me until this mission is over. If, in His divine plan, more could be accomplished by my no longer being in the picture, then that is okay too. I will be able to say as did the apostle Paul in Romans 14:8, 'If I live, I live unto the Lord. If I die I die unto the Lord; therefore whether I live or die, I am the Lord's.' So you see, my dearest angel, being careful is not a part of the program. The next couple of weeks we will establish a plan with definitive goals, ever-flexible to the leading of our great God. He allowed us to make more great contacts today than I expected. We learned more about the area than I ever dreamed we would. To me this is a confirmation that we are doing what He wants us to do. I felt His guidance today in such a marvelous manner. My faith in Him has been deepened, and my determination hardened. Bless the Lord, oh my soul!"

When the time came for Katie to return to her clinic, Elmer escorted her back to her car in the parking lot. When they got there, this giant of a man stood in middle of the parking lot, head tilted up looking toward the heavens, eyes filled with tears, arms raised as though he was reaching for the stars. With a booming voice Elmer's thanksgiving and praise rolled across the college campus so loudly that other students and staff out of curiosity came walking toward them in the parking lot. Even Dr. Price was among them. Katie got in her car and drove off. Elmer climbed in the old truck, waved at the bystanders, and drove off in the other direction. Those left in the parking lot wondered, *What in the world was that all about?*

The next day again in the parking lot, Ira and Elmer were talking with Dr. Price and Katie, who had arrived early to attend one of the Bible classes in which she was enrolled.

"The first thing is to contact the Realtor. Let's see. What did I do with his name? I thought I wrote it down, but what did I do with it? We need to see what kind of arrangements we can make for using the building and adjacent lots in that square block," declared Elmer.

"I've got it," said Ira in a soft voice. "Katie just gave it back to me after she notified her contact about the boxes in the building." He pulled out the small notebook and read, "Bradshaw Reality and Property Management."

The word of their work in the inner city had reached the ears of all the students. Whenever this little group was together, it would bring a crowd, as they wanted to follow the events that took place so that they could pray for Elmer's success with his ministry.

"Elmer, it looks to me as if you have drawn an audience again. You need to share with them what has been accomplished so we can get a special prayer group going. I think we are going to need lots and lots of prayer support," noted Dr. Price.

Elmer turned to Katie and said, "Dr. Katie, you and I will go to your office and call Bradshaw."

As the two turned toward her office, Ira remarked that he had all the work he could handle over the weekend. He would be burning a lot of midnight oil in getting a rough draft of the plans drawn up on the remodel of the interior of the building. He just hoped it will not be time wasted. *It will be*, he thought, *if we don't get the permission to use the building.* At this juncture Ira knew this really was a task of faith, for no sight of accomplishment could be seen except that God would intervene. He just prayed that God would bring the right people at the right time to the right place.

Turning back, Dr. Katie replied, "I will need the phone number. Please write it down in this little book of mine, will you, Ira? Allow me to make the appointment with the Realtor and any others who might be needed and who will free you to work on the plans. Also I would like a brief statement on how you and Elmer plan to develop the entire block."

"The entire block!" said a shocked Ira as he wrote the numbers. "You and Elmer are just plain crazy. I'm going to my room and get to work."

Elmer said, "I'm staying in the parking lot to get these prayer groups organized. You go ahead to your office and make those calls, Dr. Katie."

Katie walked to her office and stood in front of the office door, key in hand with a slight mystical, Mona Lisa-type smile on her face. She muttered to herself, "This is going to be so sweet."

The Realtor was not the first call she was going to make. That one would be to Mr. Reeding, and then she would make one to Mr. Bradshaw.

Before Katie picked up the phone, she drew a deep breath and prayed, "God, first I want to thank You for the fantastic way You have opened doors that no set of circumstances or people could have opened. Now God, give me wisdom as I make these calls. I am in much need of Your guidance. I fully trust in You to open or close doors in Your divine wisdom. May all that we ask be to glorify Your Son. Amen."

She stared at the phone in her hand for a few seconds and began to press the numbers of the first call.

The warm soft voice of Rose Reeding greeted her with, "Hello?"

Katie answered, "This is Doc Katie. Is William available?"

"No, he is in Canada on business until Tuesday around noon. Anything I can do?" replied Rose.

With a big smile on her face, she said with no small measure of excitement, "Great! Timing couldn't be better. If William is not too tired, could the two of you give me a couple of hours of your time Tuesday evening? I want to share with you something that I think will be of great interest to you."

"My, my, Katie, this must be something important, the way you sound. Do you want us to help plan your wedding? I can't think of anything that would make a rather reserved gal like you so excited," Rose said and giggled. "Come at four, and we will all have dinner at six and have time after dinner to talk some more if needed. William won't be too tired, I assure you."

"Oh, that's great. I'll see you at four Tuesday afternoon, and no, it's not about me. I'm quite content the way I am for now. Too many irons in the fire to be bogged down with a man. This is so much bigger and better than anything about me, I assure you, and thanks," said Katie.

As she hung up the phone, Katie said to no one but herself. "Well, that's one phone call. God, I want to thank You for keeping the door open. Now for a call to Mr. Bradshaw."

"Bradshaw Realtor and Property Management, how may I direct your call?" inquired the receptionist.

Katie responded, "May I speak with Mr. Bradshaw? I'm Dr. Katie Koch."

"I'm sorry, Dr. Koch, but Mr. Bradshaw is out of town and will not return to the office till Wednesday morning at 8:30 a.m. Is that too early?" asked the receptionist.

"Wonderful, please make an appointment for us to see him at 8:30 Wednesday, and thanks much." Katie hung up and turned from her phone. She thought, *So far so good, and thanks, God, for keeping the door open. Now I need to see Elmer. I hope he is still out in the parking lot, organizing the prayer groups.*

Katie was deep in thought as she left her office and turned when *bam!* She ran into someone or something so hard that she lost her balance and all but knocked the breath out of her. She felt two hands on her waist that not only steadied her but lifted her off her feet and then set her down so gently. His hands remained on her waist to give her balance.

Big Elmer looked down as Katie was looking up to see whom she had run into. Their eyes met. Katie had seen that look in Elmer's eyes before—when his eyes met hers as they were pulling him out of the ring on that fateful night and again a couple of hours later when he came into the waiting room of a hospital. Eyes of fear, eyes of deep compassion, eyes of sorrow, eyes of guilt, eyes filled with a desire to make amends, eyes of a big man carrying a bigger burden than his own strength could handle, eyes of a man consumed with the desire to take the hurt and pain of others and make them his own no matter the inconvenience or personal cost. The scripture verse found in Hebrews 12:2 came to mind. *For the joy that was set before Him, He endured the suffering and shame of the cross. No wonder we see God opening doors for Elmer, for he is walking in the footsteps of Jesus*, thought Katie.

Elmer was the first to speak. "Oh, I'm so sorry. I'm so sorry. Did I hurt you? Are you all right? It's all my fault. I wasn't looking where I was going. I'm just an oversized, clumsy galute."

"Oh stop it! I'm fine. I'm fine. I was looking to see you but not quite that suddenly," she answered. "I have some good news. We have an appointment with the Realtor, Mr. Bradshaw, a week from Wednesday morning at 8:30 at his office. I'll meet you there and be a few minutes early. Be sure Ira brings the drawings he is working on."

Elmer, still with his hands on her waist, lifted her way up with extended arms, never looking away from her, and said, "Oh, that is wonderful. You, Miss Katie, are wonderful. When the first time you and your dad talked with me, I knew He had sent His angels to minister to me, and what a beautiful angel He sent!"

Dr. Price, who had arrived unseen behind them and had witnessed the collision; had his arms folded over his chest and said in slow, dry voice, "Elmer, I'm not too sure all angels can fly. I think it would be wise if you let this one stand on her own two feet, and I am confident she is now capable of doing that."

Elmer glanced in surprise over at Dr. Price and muttered, "Oh, oh, yes." As his face became a brilliant red, he quickly set Katie back on the ground.

"Well," said Katie. "That was some ride. I always wanted to know what a high school cheerleader felt like. That was so much better than any roller-coaster ride I've been on. Gentlemen, my hair must be a mess. I need a restroom to freshen up a bit. See you later."

"Elmer, there is one thing you don't lack, and that is enthusiasm. Yes, sir, this has been some kind of a day!" said Dr. Price as the two walked back to the parking lot arm in arm.

That evening as Elmer was watching the main TV news, he heard a story about an operation of the FBI along with the navy and Coast Guard. They had broken up a large gun-running scheme that had been exchanging guns for narcotics. The news went to great length to tell of the activities on the dock and the capture of a ship just off the coast in one of the biggest gun-running and dope busts. The department had learned much information as to those behind this ring, and further arrests would be forth coming. Elmer knew this event had a connection with the boxes he and Ira had seen in the building across the street from the café, and he thanked God for Dr. Katie's quick response and her connection with the right authorities.

CHAPTER 10

The next morning as Elmer was reviewing the story about the gun bust printed in the morning paper, his mind centered on upcoming activities. He was wondering how Ira was coming along with the remolding of the big building now that it was empty.

"Ira, it is just three days before we meet on Wednesday morning with Katie and the Realtor, and boy, do we ever have a lot to do. Let's start out by going and visiting Ross and Sandy again," Elmer stated in an enthusiastic voice.

"Sorry, Elmer. Can't do it. I've got the plans all but done, just a few finishing touches left, and I'm so behind with my schoolwork. I've just got too much catch up work for me to go anywhere. You will just have to solo," Ira firmly replied.

"That's fine, Ira. I'll just go on my own this time. I'll let you know how it went when I get back," said Elmer.

Elmer climbed into the old pickup and headed toward the Main Street Café to reassure Ross and Sandy that progress was being made.

He thought to himself. *God, I don't know why I'm going alone today. But I know You do, and if that's Your will, that's fine with me.*

When Elmer entered the café, he saw that Sandy was serving two customers at the counter and that two of the nine booths were filled. One had two young couples, and in another booth Ross and the two men who had been with him the first time he and Ira came to the café were sitting. One man, whom Elmer considered the boss, was angry, as his body language sent that message loud and clear. Ross had his arms folded across his chest and had a stubborn, defiant expression on his face. The other man, whom Elmer considered the goon, was leaning forward, his right hand slipped under his suit lapel and resting over his heart like he was saluting the flag, but Elmer knew his hand was on the handle of a gun.

Elmer slowly walked over to Ross and said in soft, unemotional voice, "Ross, these two fine-looking gentlemen aren't causing you any trouble, are they?"

Before Ross could answer, the boss blurted out. "This is none of your business, buster. Who in the blue blazes are you?"

Elmer stared deeply into the boss's eyes answering. "Sir, corrections need to be made regarding your statement and question. My name is not Buster. It is Big Elmer. My friends just call me Elmer, but for now you address me as Big

Elmer. As to the question regarding my location, I can and will most gladly respond. I'm not somewhere in blue blazes. I should be, but the boss of all bosses has delivered me from enduring the agony of hell. It is His gift to me, and I accepted that gift when I became aware of it. And it comes with a great guarantee that I will never be found in hell as long as I keep Him as my boss. If I had not found this boss, I would be frying in blue blazes, and I may be so unlucky as to have you as my roommate. So as to my name and as to my location, you are wrong. As to this not being my business, it most assuredly is my business because Ross is in my boss's employment. His boss has afforded him more riches in three minutes than he could ever make in three years as your pimp. But it is not the money that enlisted him. It was the assurance that he would do nothing illegal or anything that would offend our boss. We are always eager to tell our friends or a stranger about our boss and identify Him. We no longer need to feel trashy or guilty about our employer. Tell me, can the two of you say that about your boss, and how does your boss make you feel?"

The two men sat there looking dumbfounded, thinking, *How could this ugly brute of a man speak so eloquently?*

Elmer again spoke up, "Now it's my turn to ask the questions. Just nod yes or no, okay?" Up and down nods or sideways, okay? "Married? Children? Good. Now I want you to think about these last questions before you give an answer. Say your child comes home from school with this problem. All the kids in the class are to tell the class what their father does for a living—not where he worked or who he worked for but just the type of work he does. How would you answer them? Would you tell them the truth that you are a pimp who hustles others to be pimps for other pimps who are higher up the ladder than you, or would you tell them a lie so they could tell their class your lie? Days, months, maybe years later they will find out you were living a lie. You will have forever lost their trust in you. Their love will turn to utter dismay. What are you going to say to them then? I can show you a way to get out of living in a lie that you know deep in your heart is disgusting. Will you let me tell you all about my boss? The next step is yours."

The two men stood looking down, and then they looked at each other. But their eyes never turned toward Elmer. They gave no response.

Elmer seized the moment, and in a soft but commanding voice, he began to speak. "Silence is consent. Now listen to me, for I'm going to share with you the most fantastic series of events that ever occurred in human history and how you can cash in on rewards you never thought possible."

For the next twenty minutes Elmer told them of God's great love and the gift of grace that could wash away all guilt and shame and cause them to live lives that their wives and children could proudly share with them. Elmer concluded with this statement of fact: "You can continue walking down the road of life and living a lie in guilt with no self-respect and in constant fear of the mob, hoping that your wife and kids will never find out who you really are and what you really do. Or you can chose to walk in the pathway of God's love and grace. I'll be here to share more with you of the truth that will lead you to the life that is rich with God's presence. When you do God's will God's way, God blesses. You have taken one step. Now the second is yours to take. It's the big one. Give it lots of thought."

The two men looked at each other and then turned to Elmer and then looked back to each other three or four times, never saying a word. The boss took out his notebook and wrote a lengthy note and then gave it to the goon, who read it. The goon bowed his head, took three or four deep breaths, nodded his head in an affirmative manner, and then gave it back to the boss, who in turn gave it to Elmer.

As Elmer read the note, he paused and looked at the two men and smiled. A grave expression crossed his face. He looked intently at them and mouthed the words, "Are you sure?" Their body language gave no doubt they were sure. Elmer went over to them both and gave then each a big hug. No words were spoken. There was just a wave of the hand. They walked out, got in their car, sat there for a few minutes, and wrote notes back and forth, but neither said a word. They got out of the car and went back into the restaurant.

Meanwhile, in the restaurant Elmer turned to Ross and saw that his face and shirt were wet with sweat. The other customers had left, and Sandy was standing against the wall, hands folded over her heart.

Ross was the first to speak. "I could only believe what I saw because I saw it. Elmer, you're the first man I know of that has stood up to the mob, and you did more than that.

You brought them to their knees. You humbled them. They left here like whipped dogs."

"The best way to bully a bully is to bully him. Hit them where it will cause the greatest pain, and that is to their pride, their ego. When their ego is strip away and they see who and what they really are, well, that's humbling. Then I told them about Jesus. That's all I did. They and our great God did the rest," replied Elmer.

Wild-eyed, an old man named Eddie came crashing through the door and yelled, "Ross, Ross, Sandy, are you all right. I saw these two hoods from the mob come in cocky as a rooster, and then in about fifteen minutes this big guy came. And I just knew that they were going to do you in. But when they left, they looked like they had been hit by a Mack truck. What happened? Tell me what happened."

"Eddie there is no one better to tell others what went on in here than you. Sit down this may take a few minutes," replied Ross.

Elmer turned and spotted Sandy. She had come out from behind the counter and was standing against the far wall, hands to her face. When she saw Elmer coming toward her, she ran to meet him and flung herself into his massive arms.

"Oh, thank God you came, Elmer. They were really putting the squeeze on Ross." Sandy spoke softly and continued in the same soft voice, "There will be a contract out on the two of you. The mob can't afford to let you get away with this. If they do, there will be a real big rebellion against them, and they'll lose control of this neighborhood.

What happened may not be as good as we think. The arms of the mob extend to the state capital and even to Washington. I'm worried sick."

Elmer took both of Sandy's hands and held them ever-so-gently as he spoke to her. "Sandy, our boss has His people in the state capital and in Washington and somewhere that the mob has no representation, and that is before the throne of God. As we trust in Him, He will send us the help we need. Our God will not fail us! He will provide! We need to be patient and wait for Him to act. Let's place our trust completely in Him."

Sandy looked at him shyly and said, "I only feel safe when you are around."

Elmer encouraged her and built up her confidence in God by stating, "Sandy, you can do it! When you go home, go to bed and read the all seventeen verses of Psalm 40 slowly. Drink in the words. Then read it again and look for a couple of verses that really speak to your heart. Read it a third time and meditate on each promise He makes. You will wake up in the morning with a spring in your step, with confidence to meet whatever the day may bring, and oh, will you promise me to tell Ross to do the same thing?"

Sandy nodded her head eagerly as she looked trustingly into his eyes, and then her countenance turned again to fear. The two hoods had returned from the car.

They walked straight toward Elmer, the boss a step ahead of the goon. The boss held out his hand to Elmer, and with a half smile on his face and in a quiet but firm voice, he said, "We want to take you up on your invitation to hear more about your boss. My name is Vic, and my partner is Mike."

Elmer stepped forward, and with both his hands he smothered Vic's hand in his.

For the next forty-five minutes they talked. Vic and Mike asked question after question, and Elmer kept telling them that the walk with Christ was a walk of faith and trust. "We don't know what God has in mind for us, but we have faith to trust Him that He will guide and protect us. We must make a commitment to Him, willingly obey His teachings, and fully believe that He will keep His promises," Elmer said confidently.

Elmer prayed with them that God would give them the courage to walk through a valley where the shadow of death would be ever-present. Elmer gave them each a hug as they left. Elmer's thoughts were on the men, knowing they would be starting on a new path in life. Vic and Mike also knew they had a lot of cleanup work ahead of them. They were both ready to get with it.

Vic and Mike got into their car but did not leave right away. Instead they wrote notes back and forth to each other.

Eddie, too, left as though he was a man with a mission. Eddie was the town gossip. In an hour's time everyone in the area would know what had occurred at the Main Street Café along with plenty of embellishments. Eddie seeing Vic and Mike's car still at the curb walked over to it and asked, "Where are you guys going?" Vic wrote a note and handed it to Mike, who read it, nodded his head up and down, and passed it to Eddie. The note said, "We are bugged. We have a lot of information we want to tell the authorities."

Eddie grinned, reached into his back pocket, pulled out his wallet, opened it, and showed it to Vic and Mike. Looking pleasantly surprised, they motioned for Eddie to get in the backseat when they saw his FBI badge. Mike said to Vic, "Elmer's boss sure works fast." They left and then headed to the offices of the FBI. Eddie would show them the way.

With a slight smile on his face, Elmer turned to Ross and Sandy and asked, "Ross, how many men and women are there in this area who are trained in a profession but for some reason lost their desire to live that type of life and have gone to drink or something worse and given up trying?"

Ross was silent, deep in thought, and then he said, "Just about everyone who is living in this district is here because of some heartache or trauma, or they grew up here and feel trapped and can't see a way out."

Elmer asked another question. "Do you think some are here because of their own sin and folly and others may have lost it all for being blamed for another's greed?"

Ross had a sad look in his eyes and agreed. Elmer continued, "Do you think maybe some got railroaded out of the circle of the so-called honest society and they can't trust the outside world?"

Ross stared in excitement at Elmer, who seemed to have a picture of life on this side of town, and said, "That's why folks here formed their own little society and look out for one another and take care of each other."

Then Ross looked skeptical and added, "We just don't trust outsiders or the do-gooders who want to bring us back to the honest society. No thanks. Been there, done that. Worn that hat."

Elmer's eyes softened, and he said, "Yes, I can understand where you are coming from."

Ross continued, "We have an unofficial counsel of about seven or eight of us who get together once a month or more and talk over what's going on in the neighborhood. Elmer, we know a lot about you."

Elmer looked surprised and asked, "You do?"

Ross nodded. "Yep, we know that it was a lot more than the events of your last wrestling match that drove you from the ring. You weren't happy about the fixing of matches, the corrupt politics, and dishonest hype that goes along with the game. While you might make a hundred thousand, others were making ten times that amount by all kinds of illegal means. Elmer, you wanted out but felt trapped. I'm right, aren't I?"

Elmer nodded, listening intently. Ross went on, "There is just one thing we can't figure out. If you are here to bring us back into the outside way, then you had better leave … like now. If not, then why are you here spending your time and money on us?

Elmer was taken aback by all this. As he looked at Ross, he saw a truly honest man who had a deep, deep love and understanding for his neighborhood and also one who did his homework.

Ever-so-carefully Elmer chose his words. "Ross, you are right about my wanting to leave the ring. I was becoming very, very uncomfortable, and I did feel trapped. I saw no way out. Even when I heard that horrible sound of the bones being broken and the death cry of a good, clean young man, I did not know that was the door opening for my way out. I felt even more trapped. I felt strongly that I had to go to the hospital, and when I was about to enter, fear crept into my heart, telling me to turn back, and I did. There I saw an answer, a neon sign across the street blinking on and off, flashing the word *bar*."

Ross was surprised that Elmer had even thought of going to the hospital and even more surprised that Elmer had stopped when he had spotted a bar close by. He interrupted Elmer by asking, "Did you go to the bar? That's where I would have headed!"

Elmer shook his head and answered, "Ross, if I followed that light, I would always be led by the darkness of guilt and shame. I knew there must be some other way. I turned again to the doors of the hospital, not really knowing any of the why, what, when, where, or how to find an answer ... or if there even was an answer. All I knew was that I was doing the right thing. I was heading in the right direction. Inside that hospital God had already brought the right people. He set the table for me to find the answer. And I did. Oh yes, I found more than I could ever have hope for or expected—to the light that would clean and guide me, to the only one who had the answer, God."

Elmer paused. He could tell that Ross was feeling uncomfortable now with his story. He asked Ross. "Did you want to say something?"

Ross nodded with downcast eyes and asked, "How can God clean you and guide you? Is He really the one who has all the answers?"

Elmer's eyes lit up, and he said eagerly, "Yes, oh yes. From that time on I wanted to follow His leading. He has a goal He wants me to reach. I'm not there yet, so I'll just press on, and He will show me when I have reached it. Ross, I'm here because I want to tell one and all that God has never stopped loving them and is a forgiving God and will bless them if they will do His will His way, for He has a plan for their lives. All they need to do is to allow Him to guide them and to follow that guidance. I am here because I desire with all my heart for them to find the freedom that I found. Whether they remain in this area or not is not my concerned. That's between them and God."

They both stood looking at each other and smiled. Ross gave a nod of his head but said nothing.

"I'm going to see Mom and Pop. I need a few groceries," said Elmer as he turned and left.

CHAPTER 11

Things weren't going well inside Mom and Pop's store. A young man had parked his motor scooter in front of their store and had gone in with a worried look of desperation on his face. In a slow and trembling voice he declared to Mom that his mother was very ill and that they needed some food. The doctor said she could only eat soft food, and he didn't know what the doctor meant.

"Isn't most all food soft after its cook?" he asked Mom.

Mom was smiling as she wrote out a note and handed it to Mae. She read the note. Then Mea took four medium-sized paper sacks and an empty box, placed them in her grocery cart, and scooted off to fill the order.

"What you will need is some cottage cheese, puddings, instant powdered potatoes, oatmeal, and Jell-O. The instructions are on the boxes, and you'll need to put the cottage cheese in the refrigerator. I don't know if you should add some soups or not. They may have too much salt in them for her. Now when you get home, call the doctor and see if this is what he had in mind, and oh, ask him about the soup, okay? Now about you—When did you eat last? You look a little green around the gills," said Mom in a soft, understanding voice.

Mom continued talking to the young man. "What's your name?" she asked.

"Hal— No, I mean Chuck," he replied.

Something is not right here, thought Mom. "Well, I'm going to call you Hal since you don't seem too sure because many years ago when I was in the fifth grade, I had a crush on a boy named Hal. Of course he never knew it, but to this day Hal has been one of my favorite names. So Hal it is. That's what it is too, isn't it?" Mom asked softly.

Hal's mind was spinning. *She is just like my grandmother. She always knew when I was lying and seemed to be able to see right through me. How am I going to answer her?* he wondered.

Just as Hal had gathered himself, with a glare on his face he leaned forward a bit to respond to Mom. Mae returned with his order. She didn't have the space she needed to unload the cart, so she stepped between the cart and Hal, shot out her hip, and gave him a big push down the counter toward the door. Her back was now toward Hal.

Hal was confused. He felt boxed in. His first and only priority was his mother, and he would do anything to bring her food and medication. Anything! Anger swept through him. He turned, grabbed Mae around the waist with his right hand, and yanked her body tightly against his, his left hand going quickly under her arm and reaching for her wrist. He shoved Mae's hand over her mouth and nose. She could hardly breathe. Mae's eyes were wide and filled with fear. Hal pinned her against the counter, releasing his hand from around her waist. He reached into his pocket and pulled out a small revolver. With a shaking hand he pointing it toward Mom and yelled at her that he needed money and medicine for his mother.

He drew a big breath. He was just beginning to realize what he was doing, and in an almost apologetic voice, he said, "It's just got to be this way."

With a quiet, soothing voice, Mom replied, "No, Hal, it doesn't have to be this way. God has a better way, a right way, and we can work it out. Just let go of Mae and put the gun away, and I'll—"

Before she could finish speaking, the little bell at the door of the store rang, telling one and all that someone was entering. Big Elmer filled the doorway, his head almost touching the top of the door and his broad solders just missing the door jams. With his head slightly bowed, he took a full step inside before he looked up. Then he froze as he looked over the situation. Hal had turned toward the door, pulling Mae with him. And as he did, his left hand lowered a bit, and Mae took a long, deep breath. At the sight of Big Elmer Hal's hand and gun shook even more than before, and he stared in awe at this huge man.

As Hal turned, his hand over Mae's face slipped, and she took full advantage of the situation and bit down as hard as she could on the upper part of his thumb. Her bottom teeth tore into the tender meaty part of his hand as her upper teeth were fastened onto the bone that joined the thumb to the hand. The grip was solid.

Hal let out a cry of pain. Elmer saw that Hal's attention had been diverted from him and took one stride with his right foot. His left foot moved up with the grace of a ballerina, and Elmer's foot hit the gun that was still pointed at him. A shot rang out as the gun went flying into the air and landed on the counter in front of Mom.

Elmer's head jerked to the right. He lost his balance and fell into a fifteen-foot-long shelve of canned goods and other items that ran parallel to the checkout counter. The shelf was barely able to withstand the onslaught of Elmer's weight, but the contents weren't. Cans of beans, peas, and corn came cascading down along with the relish, mustard, catsup, and pickles. It was the pickles and catsup that careened on Elmer's head simultaneously, both bottles breaking and pouring out their contents over his wounded skull. He felt that he was back in the ring—the smells, the yells. As each can hit the floor, it sounded to him like the count of a referee, and then there was blackness. The big guy fell into unconsciousness. Hal dropped Mae and ran to Elmer's side. He was the first to reach Elmer. Hal was crying. "I'm sorry. I didn't mean to hurt you. Oh, I'm sorry. Oh, I've killed you! I've killed you. Your brains are all over the place!"

The young lad began shaking and sobbing so hard that now his words were all garbled and no one could understand what he was saying.

Mom ran over to where Elmer had fallen and wrapped her arm around Hal and tenderly said, "Now, now Hal, get a hold of yourself. That's not his brains you see. That's pickles covered with catsup. Look, he's moving!"

Mae's head had been just two or three inches from the gun when it had fired. Mae sat up from the floor where Hal had dropped her, scooted over to the checkout counter, and leaned back against it. She placed her hands over her ears, pressing them hard against her head. In her head the computer called the brain was having all kinds of problems calculating the seemingly thousands of sounds that were pouring into it. For more than eight years it had known only the serenity of silence, and now there were shrills. Thunder like the Tower of Babel had come to visit. A thousand voices, some sopranos, others altos, tenors, and basses all in different keys, all at different tempos. Gone, gone was the sweet peace of silence.

CHAPTER 12

The emergency room at the hospital had three new patients entering at the same time and two more patients on the way. The big guy was a sight to be seen only at a Halloween party. They had to pick a lot of glass out of his skull, and the MRI indicated a concussion. Plus he needed a few stitches where a bullet had scorched his head, taking some hair and breaking skin above his ear. He would be a resident of the hospital for a few days or until he was no longer dizzy when he moved.

The much younger man had to receive several stitches in his hand because of a wound from a bite, and he would be released later that day.

A young girl was immediately sent to a hearing specialist who quickly determined her hearing had partially been restored. She was to undergo rehabilitation to allow her brain to adjust to sounds and help speak in an understandable way. No time estimate was given.

An elderly lady with her husband had closed their grocery store even before they could clean up a big mess because she had a throbbing headache. Her eyesight was blurred, and there were black dots racing around, darting across the pupils of her eyes. Her blood pressure had shot up through the roof. She had arrived just in time to avoid a massive stroke. With medication doctors were able to bring her blood pressure down to an acceptable level. She would remain in the hospital overnight for observation.

The last to be admitted was a lady in her early forties in the last stages of terminal cancer. Her son, who now donned a heavily bandaged left hand, was by her bedside day and night for the last six days of her earthly life.

While still in the hospital Big Elmer wrote in his daily journal that Ira brought to him.

> Each person has their own set of circumstances to face, their own journey to walk, and their own life to live. We can choose to take this walk of life in our own power, trusting in our judgment, being guided by our own wisdom only to be faced with the changing winds of new circumstances, some of which would blow us off course. And at times we are unable to find a way to get our lives back on a sure track. We will be ever-seeking, ever-searching, but never quite able

to find the peace, fulfillment, and stability for which we are longing. We will always be walking in the shadows of our past. Or we could choose to accept the opportunity that God offers us, to place our hand in the hand of His only begotten Son. He faced every temptation known to us and was never moved from the course His heavenly Father had set for Him. He overcame every negative circumstance, even death. Victory was His because He did God's will God's way, and God blessed Him. God also promises this to those who are His children. God's grace coupled with our faith leads us into an overwhelming light that will dissipate all the shadows of our yesterdays. This I believe to be true. Now I must ask myself a question, "Why am I still haunted and hounded by a shadow from the past?"

CHAPTER 13

It was Tuesday afternoon when Dr. Katie and Ira entered the home of the Reedings. Ira was a bit awed by its size and splendor and began to doubt that the humble plans that he had drawn up. Although Ira had worked hard on them, he wasn't satisfied with them. He felt this was his baby, and he just couldn't get it perfect enough in the rough draft. Also he wondered if their plans of developing the complete block would seem too much for the Reedings to picture all at once. *Will our dreams of reaching that blighted area of town with the good news of Christ and raising the self-esteem of those who lived in the area come to an end?* Ira thought.

The gentleman who answered the door greeted Katie with a big smile and said, "It's always good to see you, doctor. Mr. and Mrs. Reeding are waiting for you in the sitting room."

William and Rose stood up, and Rose walked over to Katie. They gave each other a big hug. Ira could tell right way that they were the best of friends.

William then greeted Katie, after which he turned to Ira and said, "So you're Ira. I've heard so much about you and your big friend, and now I have the privilege of meeting you. What a pleasure. I have seen Elmer but have never been introduced to him. I understand the two of you want to develop some property I own and have some plans for me to approve, am I right?"

Ira was completely taken back by what he had heard. He was confused. He looked to Katie for help. She had a smirk on her face and a twinkle in her eye as though she had just pulled a fast one on Ira and Elmer, and boy, she sure had. Had she ever!

After he regained a little bit of composure, Ira turned to Mr. Reeding and spoke with a condescending tone. "We didn't know that you were the owners of the property. We have an appointment with Mr. Bradshaw tomorrow morning to see if we could get an interview with the owner to lease the property and go from there as far as the Lord would lead us. I came here this afternoon because Dr. Katie told us how your corporation gave grants to worthy causes that would benefit the community and what we would have to do to make an application for such a grant. That's why I brought these rough plans with me."

"Well, we'll see," said Mr. Reeding. "Let me take a look at your plans, see what you've got."

There were four pages. The first page was an overall look of how the development would appear—where the buildings would be located and what they would house. The second page contained the inside details of the present structure—the restaurant, the shops, restrooms etc. The third showed the training schools facing 6th Street and the shops taking up half of 5th Street. The fourth page showed the memorial chapel that would seat 350 people.

To Ira it seemed like Mr. Reeding stared at those four pages for hours, but it only lasted about twenty minutes.

Finally Mr. Reeding lifted his head, sat up straight, and looked at Ira. He smiled and said, "Interesting, interesting concept. I really like it. But it looks to me you're trying to place twenty pounds of goodies into a five-pound sack. Ira, the building department will never give you a building permit on this layout. The first reason and question they will raise is this: 'Where are people going to park their cars?' This just won't work in this small an area. We will have to move the chapel and the training center."

"No, wait. Those are the two most important things. Without them it's just another run-of-the-mill shopping area," Ira pleaded.

"Ira, you are so right," said Mr. Reeding. "So let's make them the most important. And here is how we will do it. Do you remember nearly seven years ago when this area was the center of the riots in our city? Block after block was torched, and the firemen could not fight the flames because the rioters posed a danger to them. So when the smoke had cleared, the banks found that they held mortgages on worthless, barren properties. Insurance companies were overwhelmed by claims. I and nine other prominent investors formed a property syndicate called Golden Acres. In negotiations with the banks and insurance companies we bought up all the properties we could lay our hands on. We hired Mr. Bradshaw to manage the properties. The first three years things went fairly well, but we could not entice any businesses to come into the area. Banks would not issue loans. Nor would insurance companies issue policies, so we hit a brick wall. We have had a great number of suggestions, but none seemed viable until I looked at yours. Ira, I think we can make this work."

Ira then interrupted, "Oh, Mr. Reeding, you are wrong. No, I mean you are right."

With a chuckle Mr. Reeding said, "Ira, tell me where I'm wrong and tell me where I'm right."

Ira gathered his composure and answered, "With all due respect, sir, you are wrong because what you see was not my idea. It is Big Elmer's dream and plan for making life better for the residence in this blighted area. Sir, you are right this will work. Elmer and I are sure it will. We know God loves those whose lives have been hurt and hope burned out of them. They are like these lots that you have bought. They, too, lay in ruin, filled with rubble that are reminders of the disappointments that overwhelmed them. They long to be cleaned but don't know how. We know the power of the gospel that tells us of the cleansing power of God's gift that will give to them a newness of life. Without the restoration of people it is a waste of time to restore property, for in short order they will have reduced our efforts back to ruin. On the other hand, the new person in Christ must have an outlet for making a positive contribution to the welfare of others. This is why I drew the plans and why we made an appointment with Mr. Bradshaw for tomorrow morning to see if we could lease the building and the empty block where the building stands. We had no idea you were the owner."

With a somewhat know-it-all smile and a twinkle in her eye and a humble demeanor, Katie said in a soft voice, "Ira, it had to be this way. You know the guilt and self-abasement Elmer is carrying around. Even though he is a great, devout giant of a Christian, he cannot rid himself of the guilt of causing Billy's death and the pain he caused the Reeding family. This haunts him like a shadow always following him. He struggles to believe the Reedings could ever forgive him, even though they told him so the night of Billy's death. Elmer has not seen them or spoken to them since that horrible night. To Elmer that kind of forgiveness is just impossible."

Katie paused, looked at Mr. Reeding, and continued, "I know that soon he will find out where you fit into this project, but it is how we tell him that is the problem. I'm afraid when he knows, he will just drop the whole thing and walk away, thinking God has played a terrible trick on him. I don't know where the path he would walk goes, but it would not be a good path at all. I don't know what to do. I have so much respect for him."

"I know what to do," replied Mr. Reeding with a strong, reassuring voice. "It will take a lot of teamwork from all of us. First an update and then some assignments. Right after the riots we acquired as much land as was available, which we named Golden Acres, so we hired a property manager, Mr. Bradshaw. All went well for a couple of years. Then we started hearing rumblings because of rent increases and protection fees. My partners began to jump ship, and I bought them out. I got Mom and Pop to be my eyes and ears, and their grocery store was the ideal spot. Many of the residence of the area traded there, especially since they could get credit. I am aware of all that is happening in the area. Bradshaw was skimming funds from me right and left and cheating the businessmen of the area by charging them more rent than I had authorized plus the protection fees. Then he hooked up with organized crime, which included prostitution, gun running, and narcotics, using the building. Ira, the building you and Elmer want to use is the building that became a center for their flow of traffic. The building was a great depot. Narcotics were brought from foreign countries in exchange for the guns that were stored there. Bradshaw then had the dope pushers come buy their junk, and distribution was shipped across the nation."

"Wow, we had no idea what we were getting into," a wide-eyed, astonished Ira blurted out.

Katie then said, "True, Ira, you had no idea, but Elmer did. And he shared with me one day soon after he started Bible college. Elmer knew what he wanted to accomplish in the inner city, but he didn't know how God was going to work it out. Elmer knew that the wrestling industry was deeply infested with the mob. What he did not know was that the mob had his former manager, Hank, in the palm of their hand. They told Hank how he could make a million bucks on every one of Elmer's matches by placing a bet on the time it would take Elmer to win. Hank would tell Elmer when to take his opponent down. Elmer had no idea the amount of money being exchanged by the mob every time he wrestled. After Elmer quit wrestling, the full realization of what was going on became apparent to him."

With a slight frown on his face, Ira said, "Katie, you and Elmer have not included me in a lot of what was going on. While I feel somewhat slighted, I am starting to realize that I could not have done the work that I did in the manner that I did it had I known about the mob's involvement in everything."

Katie paused, took a deep breath, and then continued, "And that's not all. Then came the bout with Billy. Elmer was told to let the bout go the distance but to completely humiliate the kid to where he would never again get a big-time opponent. Billy was much faster than Elmer, and Elmer became frustrated. He knew he would have to slow Billy down to comply with the instructions he had received from Hank. When he got Billy in a hold, he knew he could slow him down. He overreacted, and it caused Billy's death. Then he met Jesus, which turned his life upside down. The complete whitewashing of Billy's death at the inquest at first was a puzzle to him. He spent all of six weeks in a self-imposed isolation at his mountain cabin. He slept little and ate less. Reading and studying his Bible, he anchored his newfound relationship with the Lord. With prayer and meditation he established two goals for his life. When one of these goals was met, the other would also be satisfied. The first goal was to try to make some type of atonement for Billy's death, and the second was to free as many as possible from the chains of the mob. Ira, when you and Elmer went into the Main Street Café, the wheel of evangelism started to roll. The people of the area are taking their newfound lives to others, and every time you two went into the area, more good things happened. Key people in the area were being touched by God's grace, and the influence of the mob is openly being confronted."

Mr. Reeding then spoke, "Well, Ira, that's the report and now the assignments. I have been working with the FBI for the last two years on confronting organized crime in this area. We needed just a little bit more information. It came when two of the mob's top hit men were confronted by Big Elmer at the Main Street Café. Instead of rubbing out Ross and Sandy as they were instructed, Elmer appeared, and he shared Christ with them. They went to the office of the FBI and spilled a great big can of beans. With this new information added to the volumes we have gathered, we could see all of the I's dotted and the T's crossed.

"So about two hours ago the FBI started a massive sweep through the district to get rid of the web of organized crime that has infested the area for years. Over the next three or four days there will be hundreds of arrests made not only in the Golden Acres area but also in our own city council, state legislator, and even throughout the nation. Mr. Bradshaw will be among those arrested, as he was a key leader in this area of the underground crime syndicate.

"Ira, you and Elmer unknowingly played a part in this. Elmer could not be staying in a better place than he is now. Katie, I want you to keep him in the hospital right where he is for the next three to four days. There will be a guard posted at his door, and only you and the attending staff will be admitted in his room. I do think it would be wise, Katie, if you keep away from your regular routine for the next few days, maybe stay at the hospital. Ira, will you stay with me and come to the office and help my engineering staff develop these concepts you have shown me?"

"I would be only too happy to stay with you, if you think that is necessary. Elmer and I would really like to see what the people have to say and what concepts they envision for the land. There may be those in the area who would have input and could do the work. We want to raise the self-esteem of these people and show them that the project is not something given to them but something they did. When Elmer has his heart in something, he can sell it to anyone under any conditions. It's just the way he is," replied Ira.

"You are sure right there, Ira," said Mr. Reeding with a big smile. The smile faded to a very serious expression as he continued to speak. "The time has come, the time for full disclosure. One week from now at 2:00 p.m. I want you and Katie along with Elmer to meet me and Rose at the Main Street Café. Be sure to be on time. Rose and I will be there at 3:00 p.m. Katie, you and the people of the area organize the hour between the time you and Elmer arrive and we arrive. Timing is so important, and everything needs to run like clockwork. Elmer must not know that we are coming. I want this to be a complete surprise. Katie, it will be a grand night because by God's great power and forgiving grace, we are going to witness the rolling away of shadows. You know your assignments. See you in a week. Be much in prayer, and God will bless. Oh, will He ever."

CHAPTER 14

The next three days law enforcement agencies headed by a FBI undercover agent named Eddie swept through the area, confiscating records of those who were engaged in criminal activities. The information they had obtained from Vic and Mike in exchange for immunity was both accurate and thorough, so the disturbance was minimized, and little if any resistance occurred.

The books of the cartel revealed the amount Mr. Bradshaw had cheated the businessmen out of rent and protection money during the past three years.

With this information Mr. Reeding wrote a letter of apology to all of his tenants and businesses in the area. Enclosed in each letter were two checks. One was for the total amount of the protection fees that had been extorted from them. The second check was for the difference in rent they paid to Mr. Bradshaw and the amount Bradshaw had given to him plus a reasonable amount of interest. The letters were all hand-delivered.

Well, more than a half of a million dollars came back to the area. With that infusion of capital many who had to close their doors would come back and reopen their shops. Many of the empty buildings would once again be in full operation. Those who had weathered the storm would be able to redecorate, upgrade their inventory, add new items, and hire more personnel in the coming weeks.

This was the beginning of the revitalization of a blighted area, the start of new life. The area was being born again. It was on its way to live up to its name, Golden Acres.

Dr. Katie was at the hospital to see her patients. She only had three and wanted to make Elmer her last visit. Just outside Elmer's hospital room, she paused before entering. Bowing her head, she prayed, "God, give me wisdom beyond my own. I need You to place just the right words in my mouth."

Dr. Katie entered the room with the appearance of confidence and in complete control of any and every situation that might occur. But inside she just wanted to fling herself into his arms and cry like a baby. Later maybe but not now.

"Well, how is my favorite patient doing this fine day?" she asked with a smile.

With a scowl of wonderment on his face, Elmer barked, "You know good and well how I'm doing. What I don't know is why you're keeping me here like I'm a convict in solitary confinement. No TV, no newspapers, no visitors. Tell me why."

Dr. Katie replied, "My, my, the patient is a tad grumpy this morning. Well, that's just the way we like them, for it reassures us that they are ready to be discharged. So let's see how we're doing. Oops, blood pressure is a little on the upside. Now to listen to your heart. Just as I thought, one of the tests we ran showed a small leak of the aorta valve. Another showed some blockage beginning to form in three arteries that lead to your heart. Nothing to be too alarmed about just yet. We will want to keep an eye on them. Some meds, a lifestyle and diet change will do for now."

Elmer interrupted with a subdued but huffy voice, "*Doctor*, I am glad to hear about my health, but Katie, what's going on? Something isn't normal to say the least. You know and I know that I am perfectly fine and should be going home. Please address my question."

Dr. Katie Koch turned, walked out of the room, leaving the door open, went to the nurses' station, and said something to the head nurse. Then she found Elmer's room nurse and said something to him. She came back to Elmer's room, went over to a drawer, pulled out a "do not disturb" sign, and hung it on the doorknob. Katie left the door a little less than halfway open, took the stethoscope off from around her neck, and placed it on a stand. She pulled a chair up to the bedside and announced to Elmer that Dr. Katie Koch was off duty and that she had sent a very special friend named Katie to see him.

Katie took a deep breath, looking at the ceiling. The tension in her was almost unbearable. Whispering to herself, she made one last plea, "Oh, God, help."

She looked at Elmer, and a silly little grin came on her face. Half-laughingly, she blurted out, "Elmer, with the white bandage on your head, your head on the white pillow and the sheet tucked under your chin, you look like a sweet, loveable baby doll."

This comment blindsided Elmer. He didn't know what to expect, but that sure wasn't it. Suddenly the humor of Katie's comment hit him, and the roar of his laughter could be heard rolling through the halls of the hospital. When he caught his breath, he said to Katie, "I've been called lots of things in my life, but never have I been called a baby doll. That's like comparing a hippo to a panda bear."

"Oh, I think panda bears are very adorable," quipped Katie as she removed the bandage and examined his wound. She continued, "Elmer, I want you to listen very closely to what I am going to tell you. True, you have been, as you so eloquently put it, in solitary confinement. There needs to be three more days of solitary confinement before I will release you, and when you are released, you will be free—free of the shadow that has hounded you since you quit wrestling. But before I go on, there is something I need to share with you." Before Katie could continue, she reached out with both hands, placing one under Elmer's big hand and her other on top of his. She raised his hands to her lips and tenderly kissed it.

"Elmer, please pray for me that God might give me wisdom beyond my capacity to say to you what I must say," was the request Katie softly spoke.

There was a period of silence broken by Elmer's prayer. "Oh, my great God, how I thank You that in my darkest hour when I was broken in spirit, You sent to me a beautiful angle to minister to me. She has become my most trusted and respected friend, and so God, give me the humbleness to accept whatever message she has that You have laid upon her heart, for I know it is from You and for my good. Amen."

Elmer continued, "Katie, I know that I have a deep affection for you and complete trust in you, which is growing deeper by the day. I sense that you also have strong feelings for me. So before you say a word, there is something I must share with you. Before I met you, there was no one I could trust. Even my parents were ashamed to be identified as being the ones who were responsible for my existence. No neighbors or friends were invited into see me. It was as though I was hidden away in some back closet. School was a disaster. Kids can be so hurtful by what they say to one who is a little different. No one wanted to be a friend. I quit school after the fifth grade. I wanted so much to learn that I would spend hours each day at the library where an elderly librarian, Mrs. Frazer, took note of me. She helped me with books on history, math, English, geography, and others subjects. She was always upping my grade level a little higher than my ability and challenged me to rise to the higher level. We became the closest of friends. This was my first taste of human love. When I was just turned fifteen, I had a note from her when I got to the library, a note informing me that she was not feeling well but had made an appointment for me at the local junior college to take the GED test so I would have the equivalent of a high school diploma. I felt I did really well on the test in every category. I hurried back to the library to thank Mrs. Frazer for all her help only to find out that sometime during the night she had died. My only true friend I ever had in all my life was gone. At her memorial service a Christian minister said that God had taken her. If he would have said that she had gone to be with God, I could have accepted that, but he did not say that. He said, 'God had taken her.' I was very angry with a God who would cause the death of such a wonderful person, and consequently it was God who caused me to have so much pain, sorrow, and hurt, deeper than I had ever had in all my miserable life. My anger toward the Christian's God turned to bitterness and even hatred. I wanted nothing to do with them or their God."

Elmer paused and took a deep breath. Though his eyes were open, nothing registered as to what he saw, for his brain only saw the happenings of many yesterdays. He looked squarely at Katie as though to refocus his thoughts. He saw her with her head slightly bowed, eyes closed, tears streaming over her cheeks, hands folded with her chin resting on her thumbs.

"Oh, Elmer, that must have been devastating to you to lose such an understanding person," Katie commented.

Elmer continued, "Katie, then came that fateful, life-changing night when I saw what I had caused, a broken body lying at my feet. Then I heard at the hospital those dreadful words that Billy was dead. I had caused Billy to die, not God. God took him. I had completely misunderstood. I did not comprehend the true meaning of the minister's words concerning Mrs. Frazer's passing. He was talking about a God who conquers death by receiving the dead unto life. He is the God of life, not death. It was then that my bitterness toward God and His followers melted away. But it was then also that a deep, dark shadow fell across my life that to this day ever hunts me. I had caused Billy's death, and I have experienced the pain, sorrow, and hurt that I heaped upon his family. It is a pain and sorrow deeper than they had ever experienced. It will be a lasting hurt, and I understand their bitterness and hated toward me is justified. It was more than the life I crushed out of him. It was all the dreams and hopes for their son that were also dashed. How can I ease their immense sorrow? I don't think I can ever dispel their bitterness toward me, but there must be some way I can lessen their hurt and sorrow. I think if even by chance, they would ever see me again, it would but intensify their sorrow. Their pain is the shadow that will always follow me. It's just something I will have to live with. It is a cross that is very heavy. I know that God has forgiven me and has kissed me by His grace, which is the immensity of divine love. Can that depth of divine love be matched by lowly mortals? I think not. So Katie, my loveable, godsent angel, I have too much respect and too deep a love for you to ever encumber you with my haunting shadow. Our relationship can never be anything more than it is now."

"My, my, how interesting life would become if that dreaded shadow were to be removed," quipped a smiling Katie. "I think that might be worth working on, don't you? You and I don't know the future, but God does. Why don't we trust Him to address your apprehensions?"

Katie then became very serious as she continued, "Elmer, there are four men in my life in whom I have placed my complete trust at one time or another and always my deepest respect. They are my father, Dr. Wayne, you, and the fourth one you will meet in a few days. You said that you have the deepest respect for me. Well, we're going to put that statement to a test. Elmer, for the next three days I'm asking you to do everything that I ask of you to the smallest detail without asking why or any other question. Will you promise me you will do that? If you do, just maybe, we might be able to shed enough light to dispel all shadows. After three days you will be free from your promise no matter what happens. What is your answer?"

Big Elmer ran his fingers through his hair and felt the wound, but he still looked confused. So much he didn't know, so much he felt he had a right to know, and now this request. He felt anger swelling up inside him. He wanted to lash out. *Why, why is my angel hurting me so? Or is she? Maybe she is trying to spare me of the hurt that this shadow brings.* Slowly he responded, "Katie, there is no one on the surface of this globe I would make that kind of a promise, no one except you. Yes, I promise. I will accept your terms."

Katie, stoic, showing no emotion, whipped out her cell phone, dialed in a number, and said, "Dad, I'm bringing home a houseguest who will be with us for the next three days. He is a big man with a big appetite, so throw in an extra cup of water in the soup, and we will be seeing you in about an hour or less. Thanks."

Katie stood up, turned, walked toward the door, and said, "Elmer, I'll get the discharge papers in order while you get dressed, and oh, comb your hair. It's a mess."

Looking back over her shoulder and seeing an amazed and befuddled Elmer, she barked with a commanding yet congenial tone in her voice, "Why are you still in bed? Get with it, man. Let's go home!"

CHAPTER 15

The next two and a half days went smoother than Elmer could have hoped, thanks to Pastor Koch. They had two mornings of discussing some of the deep doctrines and issues contained in the Bible. The two afternoons were rather disappointing, for Elmer could not figure out a way to beat the crafty pastor in either checkers or chess. The few games Elmer did win he knew it was by grace and not by works.

Near noon of the third day Katie came home and announced to them. "The hour of deliverance for Elmer has come, and we are going out to lunch to celebrate. All of us need to get cleaned up and dressed in our Sunday best. We need to leave the house by one thirty on the nose."

As Katie was backing out of the driveway, Elmer asked, "Katie, where are we going to dine at this hour dressed like this?"

"Oh, to your favorite restaurant," she replied with a smile.

"That doesn't tell me anything. I don't go to high-end establishments to dine, so how could I have a favorite one that would demand this attire?" asked Elmer.

"You'll see," she said with a reassuring tone.

The rest of the drive was driven in silence. At two o'clock Katie parked in front of the Main Street Café.

Elmer made a dry comment. "These are pretty fancy duds for the Main Street Café. What are we doing here, picking up someone else to go somewhere else to dine?"

Katie got out of the car and said, "Elmer, we are not going anywhere else. This is the end of the line, or it may be the beginning of the line. Time will tell, and we will see."

Elmer was totally perplexed. Pastor Koch came alongside of Katie and slipped his arm around her arm, and Elmer came along the other side of her and did the same as they walked toward the entrance of the café.

Much was running through the thoughts of Katie. *This was the time. Your operating room is before you, Dr. Katie Koch. God, we place our trust in You.* Katie had strength not only because of her great faith in God but also because on either side of her were the two men she most respected and loved. The way to cut away shadows is to intensify the light. She has done all that she could do. The rest was up to others, Elmer and God. It was time for her to step back and just watch and pray.

Ross and Sandy had jumped at the idea of giving a special testimonial luncheon in honor of Elmer and Ira.

Just a few of the hundreds of people Elmer had led to Christ since he and Ira had dared to go to the inner city with the gospel could attend because of the size of the café. Katie would know who should be there. Now was the day.

When they entered the café, they saw colored streamers hanging from the ceiling and balloons hugging the ceiling. Strings of balloons were taped to each of the nine booths. At the far end of the room and above the half-round booth was a very large image of an angel and a slightly smaller one made of white papier-mâché. On the face of the larger angel was a picture of Big Elmer's face. The face of the smaller angel contained a picture of Ira's face. Above the angels these words were written: "Elmer and Ira, Our Angels." Ross and Sandy were seated at each end of this booth. Ross stood up and let Pastor Koch, Elmer, and Katie into the booth. Elmer sat in the middle.

Those present were but a fraction of the lives transformed by Christ because of the efforts of Big Elmer and Ira. Those present included Mom and Pop, Hal and Mae, Vic and his wife and family, Mike and his wife and family, Eddie and his wife, President Tom and his wife, and Dr. Price and his wife from South Bay Bible College. All the booths were filled.

There was a table in the middle of the room midway between the counter and the big booth at the end of the room. The table was set for four people. The four chairs were empty.

Everyone but Ira was here. Elmer noticed this quickly, bent over toward Katie, and whispered, "Where is Ira? This is his ministry too. He's got to be here. This is not like him. He is so punctual. I'm worried about him."

With an ever-so-soft voice Katie responded as she tenderly patted Elmer's hand, "Be patent, my impetuous friend. Ira knows what he is doing, and he will be here at just the right time with three very important guests. I promise you that. Just trust him. Now relax, sit back, and enjoy. There are places reserved just for them."

Elmer noticed the four empty chairs and smiled and nodded, thinking to himself as he looked at her with admiring eyes, *Katie, you always have everything under control. You have never disappointed me.*

Ross, who was the emcee for the gathering, stood up and said, "Elmer, something great started right here in my little café that first afternoon you told us how Dr. Katie became your angel as she told you of God's forgiving grace and your acceptance of His gift, which completely turned your life around. Well, Elmer you came to influence my life, kind of, through the back door. I was engaged in peddling the lowest form of human behavior. You took my leading product and caused her to become an honest woman. You became her angel. When she told me how God had grafted her back into His family and I saw her transformed into a beautiful lady, I, too, wanted what she had. I accepted Him, and she became my angel. I have been an angel to others, and they in turn have helped others. Down through the centuries there are myriads of angels, people sharing their joy in Jesus. They are indeed uncountable, yet each one of us are a ministering spirit to those who await salvation.

That is our ministry, the ministry of us all. The ministry of an angel is to go tell on every mountain in every valley and at every beach that Jesus is Lord and Savior to all."

Vic and Mike shared with the group how in this very room they came to take the life of Ross and Sandy when Elmer entered. "Instead of taking lives, we found life," they said. Their wife's related how the encounter of their husbands with Jesus saved their marriages and allowed their children to have loving fathers of which they could be proud.

Eddie said, "While Elmer never personally talked to me about Christ, I heard every word that he spoke to Ross and Sandy and to Vic and Mike. As I listened, I opened my heart to Jesus. Oh, the joy that filled my life. The next Sunday I was baptized, and I knew my sins had been washed away. One might say that Elmer became my ricochet angel."

Mom, Pop, Hal, and Mae quickly followed, sharing the good that had swept through the area since the day Elmer and Ira had showed up driving that old pickup truck.

Elmer rose and said, "I was only doing what I felt Jesus wanted me to do. I have great faith in the power of the gospel, and I have a great love for the disadvantaged who are in this area. These are the two factors that motivated me to come here. The first factor is seen by your presences here this afternoon. You are a testimony to the power of the message of God's love. It is because of the magnitude of His grace, we can have such a happy and joyous meeting. The second factor, well, I'm not sure how I can tell you, for I'm not sure I understand myself, but I'll try—"

As Elmer was speaking, the chimes of the clock on the back wall sounded three times. The door of the café opened, and in came Ira arm in arm with a strikingly beautiful young lady.

Ira led Tammy Reeding to the empty table in the middle of the room with the four empty chairs and seated her in the first chair. Then He moved to the last chair, leaving the two middle chairs still empty. As Katie saw Tammy, she thought, *Thank God for a headband.* Elmer did not recognize her, for the last time he had seen her was a few years ago when she was a young teenager, emotionally crushed, sobbing uncontrollably, clinging to her grief stricken mother as they walked out of a waiting room of a hospital, leaving a dead brother and son. But he thought, *Wow, Ira, she has real class. How did you arrange that?*

As Elmer was about to continue addressing the group, the doors of the café again opened and entered a couple in their midsixties. Mr. William Reeding and his wife, Rose, walked with grace, dignity, and a confidence that came with success until they stood behind the two empty chairs, their eyes never leaving Elmer.

It took but a fleeting moment for Elmer to realize the entire Reeding family was present. The shadow of hurt and pain that had hounded him for such a long time now in an instant became in him a horrible, twisting tornado tearing away at every emotion stored in the psyche of the human brain. He knew that the shadow that followed him was not due to his pain. But it was due to the suffering he had heaped on the Reedings when they had lost their son. Elmer believed the night he accepted Christ God's forgiveness was complete. Every sin, every mistake he had made, even the causing of Billy's death was covered by the magnitude of His grace. That constant shadow was the pain the Reeding family would always have. Elmer believed they felt bitterness toward him because of what he had caused. To Elmer, that would always remain.

Elmer stopped speaking and thought, *Oh, I knew that somewhere sometime I would come face-to-face with the Reedings. But why now should they appear? Now when we are in the company of those to whom Ira and I had been such a help. Those who are the nearest and dearest to me. Now when we are all basking in the joy of Your presence in our lives. Why, why would You, God, allow them to come now?*

His heart was crying out to God, daring to question His judgments, His wisdom. With slumped shoulders, Elmer fought to analyze the situation and prayed aloud. "God, I have surrendered myself to You. You have had my greatest devotion. I labored in a vineyard of sour grapes, and You turned it into golden acres. I presented to You broken and shattered lives. You kissed them with Your grace, which transformed them into beautiful human beings. You gave them a purpose for living. My praise for You was constantly flowing from my lips. I believed that You forgave me of all my misjudgments and sins, even those that I had performed unintentionally. My causing of Billy's death, has it been excluded? Was this deed so costly that the price for my redemption could not be covered? But You God! It seems to me cannot perform your own plan?"

Elmer turned his attention toward Ira and questioned him by asking, "And you, Ira, my best friend and coworker, you brought them here? I thought I could trust you."

With a nearly broken heart, Elmer looked deep into Katie's eyes and said, "Oh, Katie, my angel, you arranged all of this? Do I find betrayal in the person I most respected?"

Both Ira and Katie, knowing what was yet to come, returned Elmer's penetrating look with a slight shy smile.

An upset and bewildered Elmer said, "Excuse me." He elbowed his way from the booth and stood in front of it so everyone could see him.

With his massive hands lightly covering his face and in a loud voice, he continued, "What is the reason to live? There is none! If true, then these eyes have seen their last sunrise. No, no, I'm confusing the situation. It is not my relationship with you, God, that I should question. It is the effect of my misdeeds. The shadow is the sorrow and sadness to others. That is what cast a shadow over my life. That is the question for which I can't find an answer. How can I ever remedy the Reeding's hurt? I have cried out to You, God, many, many times, but there is never an answer."

Elmer felt someone standing very close to him. He felt two small hands on his massive chest, sliding upward toward his face, pulling ever-so-gently. Lowering his hands and opening his eyes, he saw the face of Rose Reeding. She stood on her tiptoes and placed a tender, motherly kiss upon his lips and said just three words, "We love you." She then kissed him again as a loving mother kisses her hurting child and backed away.

Elmer could hardly remember his mother, let alone ever experiencing a mother's kiss. He knew what Rose had said came from the depths of her heart. He was stunned. His mind was in a swirl as he blurted out, "How, how could you ever love me?"

Mr. Reeding stepped forward and placed his hand on Elmer's shoulder said, "Elmer, I'll answer that question. You need to know, Elmer, that I, too, caused a person's Son to die, and because of His death, I found life. The Son's name is Jesus. Now I have a life that is abundant and fulfilling because His Father keeps pouring out blessing after blessing on me. The Father of Jesus is not angry with me. Quite to the contrary. He is very pleased with me, for when I accepted the death of His Son, that fulfilled the purpose of His Son's dying. Were it not for my son's death, you would not have accepted God's Son. You would not be the man you are today. Many in this room would not be the people they are. This community would not have had the transformation it is now experiencing. Yes, Elmer, God has used you, but He only used you because you surrendered your life to Him. You caused my son's death, and my son's death led you to accept God's Son as your Savior. When you accepted God's only begotten Son, you fulfilled the purpose for His living. In a similar manner, Elmer, with God's guidance you have honored and memorialized my son's life by giving purpose to his death. This is the answer to your question of how we can love you. Now you know that we love you deeply, even as God loves everyone who makes His Son's death worth the dying, and then He continues to lavish His grace and mercy on us. Elmer, Rose and I determined to walk in the steps of God and see that your every need would be met. Katie kept me informed of your success at Golden Acres and your dreams and plans for the development of the area. With each person you brought to Christ, our joy was every bit as yours, for we realized that our son's death had a purpose. That is the how and why we can love you. We just do!"

Elmer stood like a statue, while inside of him a great ball of peace overwhelmed his deepest thoughts and emotions, a peace that could not be described, a peace he could not comprehend, yet this peace was his to apprehend. He realized he had been wrong in thinking the Reedings were in emotional pain and distress. Oh, the greatness of God's grace! The wisdom of our great God. *All things work together for the good to those who walk in God's love. When we do God's will God's way, God blesses us. So simple to say, so rich to experience.* Above all, Elmer realized the shadow was gone. Darkness and light cannot coexist. When the light of the true emotions of the Reedings were disclosed there was no longer a shadow. The truth freed Elmer. Elmer was basking in the warm glow of complete and perfect peace for the first time in his life. Oh, how sweet it was!

The café' was filled with silence, an awe that no one wanted to break. Pastor Koch slowly stood, looked all around the room, and said, "As the years go by and we look back at this gathering, we will recall that this afternoon was one of the most inspiring and joyful times that we ever had. A fitting way to conclude our time together is to form a big circle and spend some time in expressing through prayer our gratitude to God."

When the last *amen* was said—and there were lots of hugs and good-byes—the café was empty except for Ross, Sandy, Pastor Koch, Katie, and Elmer.

Ross turned to Pastor Koch and asked, "In about six weeks could you arrange your schedule to marry Sandy and me?"

"Absolutely I can," was the reply of the smiling pastor as he shook hands with Ross and gave Sandy a big hug.

Elmer and Katie offered their congratulations.

With a clap of her hands, Sandy said, "Let's celebrate. The cook left after the noon rush, so I'll fix dinner for the five of us, and Elmer, you will not have a Ruben on rye."

Katie turned and faced Elmer. She looked right at him, trying to read any emotion that may be seen. She said in a half-serious and half-teasing manner, "Now that is so sweet, and since the subject of weddings has been brought up and you are no longer hounded by a shadow, don't you think it would be a fantastic time to continue our conversation about the future?"

In the same voice Elmer answered, "Yes, you are so right. The conversation just might be productive beyond a shadow of a doubt. Oh, Sandy, just prepare dinner for three. You all have lots of plans to talk over regarding your wedding. See you all later. God bless."

Arm in arm with a spring in their step, Elmer and Katie left the Main Street Café.